Amityville Subdivision

Brad D. Sibbersen

PART ONE
NOW/THEN

$$\text{———} \mathbf{\textit{1}}$$

The sun punched through the bedroom window, right into her eyes.

If that wasn't a clear sign that she should probably get up, nothing was.

She rolled over – groggy, hair mussed, one nightgown strap falling off a shoulder – and squinted at her alarm clock. It had stopped during the night, sometime just after three. She sighed. The power had probably gone out again. Glitchy power. No cable. No cell phone tower. The price one paid for living in a brand new development.

Well, she didn't have to be in the office at any particular time

did she?

so no harm done if she was a little "late". She stretched, popped her back, and then slid out of bed. Thirty minutes later she was showered, dressed, and had a cup of instant in her hand, day-old, reheated in the microwave. She didn't bother putting on makeup.

Jasper caught her in her driveway. Her house was the first one on the left when you entered the cul-de-sac, and his was the *second* on the left, so as her sole immediate neighbor she'd gotten to know him reasonably well. He was walking... what was its name?... Patches, his tiny little mixed-breed whatsit. She had always referred to small, yippy dogs like Patches as "Little Lord McMuffins", an appellation she was inordinately proud of. Jasper waved her over. He had gossip.

"Morning!" she said. It came out cheerier than it felt. She couldn't get her brain out of first gear, not even with the coffee. She felt like she'd been up all night.

"Morning!" he smiled back, making a beeline for her. Patches tugged at his leash. Naturally, he wanted to examine something invisible in the exact opposite direction. "They were at it again!" Jasper said conspiratorially after closing the distance between them, even though there was no one else to hear. Anyway, Robert, across the street, was mowing his lawn, making plenty of racket to drown them out.

"Your nemeses?" Abby asked, smiling.

"Oh, I'd hardly call them my *nemeses*," Jasper said with a theatrical wave of his hand. "Just neighborhood nuisances. College girls should live on campus, where they can party to their hearts' delight, not in a quiet residential neighborhood like this!"

"Well..." Abby said, looking in the direction of the house in question. She could see the roof from here, but the trees sprouting from a pair of circular, equidistant center islands blocked much of her view. There was a third island as well, smaller, triangular, located between the other two but several yards closer to the entrance. Instead of trees, this one was adorned with an array of well-maintained, colorful flowers. The foliage was pretty, yes, but to Abby's way of thinking the islands were little more than traffic hazards, obstructing your view and forcing you to drive around the entire cul-de-sac instead of just cutting across. Plus they were an irresistible lure to young drivers, who felt compelled to weave in and out of them, creating yet another hazard.

"Well, you can't blame them," she shrugged. "If I could've afforded my own place in college – my own *house* – I would've jumped at the chance. Brand-spanking-new development like this, they probably thought they'd be the only ones living here for the duration."

"Well they're not. So much racket. Music, hollering, carrying on 'til all hours. With no consideration for the rest of us. That's the problem with being born with a silver spoon up your ass," he lamented. "You don't have to work for anything, so you don't respect those who do."

Abby didn't recall hearing anything last night. Maybe, from her location, the trees blocked the noise.

"Which one of them actually owns the place

again?" she asked.

"Madison, I think. Maybe Emily. Frankly I can never remember which is which."

Emily is Buffy, Abby thought to herself, immediately wondering what the hell that even meant and where it came from.

"Morning!" someone else shouted from across the street. Robert's wife, Roberta, awkwardly making her way to her car in unfamiliar heels.

"And then there's *those* two," Jasper said, rolling his eyes dramatically. Abby snickered. Robert and Roberta Remington were a constant source of amusement, not just because of their names, but also because they bore a striking resemblance to one another. The neighborhood joke was that they were from Kentucky. "You know who they remind me of?" There was a sparkle in Jasper's eyes. "The Wonder Twins! You probably don't remember the Wonder Twins. That was before your time."

"Oh, I know them," Abby said, laughing. "Cartoon Network."

"Of course!" Jasper laughed. "Nostalgia never dies."

Patches whined at the end of his leash.

"Okay, His Majesty speaks. We must be off. Toots!"

"Toots," Abby said. She watched as he crossed the street so that the little dog could relieve itself amidst the skeleton of one of the identical properties going up across the way. Their street, at the epicenter, had been the prototype, the seven homes there the first built and first sold. The others spread out in all directions, seventeen identical cul-de-sacs in all, seven lots each, in various stages of completion. As a result, workmen and construction machinery were omnipresent five days a week, the sound of backup alarms so pervasive that her mind had reduced it to background noise.

It was a strange setup, Abby reflected as she pulled out of her driveway, eased around the corner, and drove several yards on the shoulder to give a bulldozer headed in the opposite direction enough room to pass. The houses were so samey, and yet the style the architect or the investors or whoever determined such things had settled on was oddly dated: Dutch Colonial, with a second-floor balcony facing the street and out-of-fashion quarter moon windows peering out of a sizable, third-floor attic. Jasper's nostalgia again, she supposed. Several workmen waved at her as she drove past – not because they knew her, but because she was an attractive woman – and she suffered one wolf whistle. Then she was out of the development, on the single, lengthy road that connected it to reality, and ten minutes later she reached the access road that merged onto the highway.

What did she have going on today? She couldn't even remember, so dense was her mind from lack of sleep. She needed another cup of coffee, a good one. She exited at the next ramp and pulled into the Big Guy Mart.

"The usual?" asked the man behind the counter when she walked in. She was a regular.

"Make it a double. I feel like I didn't sleep a wink last night."

"Done and done," he said. He rang her up for the double espresso while she served herself from the machine. In the process she managed to drop her lid, spill coffee on herself while picking it up, and knock over the napkin dispenser when she tried to extract one with her free hand.

"The day can only get better, right?" she laughed, ignoring the glare from the next person in line. Her antics were holding him up.

"That's all we can hope for. Six ninety-nine."

"Dingbat klutz," muttered the commuter she'd held up after she fumbled her way out the door.

"Broad's fucking crazy," the man operating the register replied. In fact, he was the owner, the Big Guy himself, and had no qualms about swearing in front of his customers. If they didn't like it, there was a Circle K next exit up.

"No doubt."

"No, I mean *really* crazy. She comes in here every morning for coffee. On her way to work, she says. Claims she works for a magazine or something. Whole cast of characters at this supposed place. But I see her car, every day, just driving back and forth, up and down the highway. For hours. Then she stops in in the evening, sometimes, and rattles on like she's been at the office all day. Crazy fucking bitch."

The commuter looked after her, watched as

she pulled out of the parking lot.

"Probably on drugs," he concluded.

"Everyone's on fucking drugs," said Big Guy.

——— **2**

"You can't park here!" barked the officer. He was discussing something with a balding, sour-faced man on the front lawn. His patrol car was idling across the street. Presumably the sour-faced man lived there.

"I don't see any signs," Abby said.

"I **said**, you can't park here!" the officer repeated, daring her to say another word.

He was full of shit, but there was no point in arguing with him. "This is what I'm talking about..." she heard the sour-faced man say as she pulled away. She drove up to the next block, turned the corner, and parked there. As she walked back, she smiled and waved at the officer. Both men glared at her.

There was another cop car in front of the address she was looking for. Two officers were just climbing out of it. There was a large, silver box truck, too, and several other cars, some few parked haphazardly on the lawn, most parked in front of neighboring homes up and down the street. Two young, muscular guys were struggling a large, draped object strapped to a pallet up the truck ramp with a pallet jack. Other people were packing or unpacking boxes, carrying electronic equipment into or out of the house, walking around with clipboards. A lot of them were college students. A Middle Eastern gentleman rushed out to meet the police officers, who'd been joined by an officious man in a brown suit who seemed to appear out of nowhere.

"This is private property!" Middle East said.

"Private *residential* property," said Brown Suit.

"Are you the owner?' asked one of the cops.

Abby recognized Middle East now. Professor Ahmad Mahmoud. He was the one she was supposed to talk to.

"We've warned you *repeatedly* about running a business out of this property when it isn't commercially zoned," said Brown Suit, shoving a sheaf of papers in the professor's face.

"I'm not running a business!" Professor Mahmoud declared, just as a large delivery truck pulled up. The driver leapt out of the cab, digital clipboard in hand.

"I need somebody to sign for these!" he shouted to no one in particular. "Sixteen crates!"

Brown Suit frowned.

"It's not a business delivery!" Mahmoud insisted. "I just buy a lot of stuff on Amazon!"

"So all these people, they aren't employees?" Brown Suit scoffed.

"Maybe it's a party," the professor suggested.

"Then we're breaking it up," said one of the cops.

Brown Suit tried, again, to force his sheaf of papers on Mahmoud.

"You'll have to serve those to my brother," the professor said, refusing to touch them. "My attorney," he clarified.

"Where *is* this attorney?" asked the other cop.

"Egypt."

"You better get him back here. You're gonna need him."

"I'll call him right now," said Mahmoud, pulling his phone out of his pocket.

Clearly this wasn't the best time. She gave the scene a wide berth, dodged a little girl carrying a stack of laptops, held the front door for a guy who was backing through it with a cumbersome cardboard box, then slipped into the house. Maybe she could locate the person she was *really* here to see.

Or maybe not. If anything, it was more chaotic inside than out.

"Are you the physicist?" a woman immediately asked her. "Or is the Japanese guy the physicist?"

"The Japanese guy," someone answered for her.

"Then please tell me you're the pizza girl."

"Uh, no."

"Well, thanks for nothing." The woman

pushed by her without another word.

The Japanese guy in question (she assumed) caught her eye. He was tinkering with some sort of electronic gizmo that wouldn't have looked out of place in a 1940s science fiction movie. "Don't feel bad," he said. "When I got here they asked me if I was delivering the Chinese food." He shook his head. "Not. Even. Chinese." A shower of sparks exploded from his gizmo. "Oh, shit!" he exclaimed, returning his attention to it.

"Do they have a warrant?" she heard someone ask. "They have to have a warrant." Another Middle Eastern guy, shouting into a cell phone. The lawyer-brother who was supposedly in Egypt?

A prim older man and a pale young woman, wisp-thin, her hair dyed silver, were staring at Abby from the other side of the room. She was clearly the subject of their subsequent exchange.

"Does anyone...?" she tried, raising her voice to be heard over the din. "I'm looking for Miss DeVries. Is Rachel DeVries here?"

"You shouldn't be here." She didn't see who said this, but she was pretty sure it was directed at her.

"You! Little Girl Lost!" A handsome, dark-haired man wearing a Kansas City Royals sweatshirt was waving her over. She had to squeeze past two oblivious college girls, eyes glued to their phones, to get to him. He extended his hand.

"Abilene Beaumont?" he asked.

"Yes, thank God!" They shook.

"That's an interesting name."

"Trust me, I've heard 'em all."

"Me too. Last name's Whiteshroud. Pawnee."

"Native American Pawnee?" she asked.

"I prefer *Indian*. No shame in that word. *Native American* reeks of condescension. 'We stole all your land, but here, we'll name you after what *we* decided to call the place.'"

"Fair enough," she smiled. "I'm glad you know me, but *how* do you know me?"

"Professor Mahmoud told me you'd be joining us. It's a bit chaotic here tonight so I took it on myself to keep an eye out for you."

"Thanks, I appreciate it."

"He's kind of tied up right now, as you might have noticed, so let me introduce you around. You drink coffee?"

"Constantly."

"Well, there's coffee. You!" He snapped his fingers at one of the cell phone girls. "I'm sorry, I don't know your name. Can you get Ms. Beaumont here a cup of coffee?"

"Right away!" the girl said, scampering off.

"*Ms*. Beaumont is my uptight, spinster, non-existent sister. Abilene, please. Abby, preferably."

"And I'm Shane," he smiled.

The girl returned with the coffee.

"Sorry, it's been reheated like a million times," she said.

"I'm not in it for the taste," said Abby, happily accepting it.

"I think it's decaf," the girl said apologetically.

"Not in this house," Shane assured them both.

"With you, we're thirteen. I hope you know that." The prim man, the one who'd been talking to the silver-haired girl.

"Excuse me?" Abby asked.

"Jasper Janowitz. We were just discussing the fact that, with you, we're thirteen. Very unlucky. Four, seven, nine, and seventeen are also considered unlucky numbers for this sort of endeavor."

"Seven?" Abby asked. "I thought that was a *lucky* number."

Jasper shook his head. "Not when it comes to ghosts, not to the Chinese."

"I'm *Japanese!*" the guy fiddling with the sci-fi gizmo interjected, obviously playing.

"Okay, so now you've met Jasper," Shane smiled. "The guy who is adamantly not Chinese is our physicist, Itsuki Kobayashi. Suki for short."

"A boy named Suki!" the physicist joked.

"Girl over yonder with the silver hair is... something Winters..."

"Winter Allegheny," Jasper provided.

"Quite the name."

"Says *Abilene,*" Jasper said, raising a single eyebrow. "Winter is one of the most powerful psychics in the country. She puts me to shame."

"Oh, you're... psychic?" Abby said. Shane rolled his eyes.

"This one's a *disbeliever,*" Jasper explained in a theatrical whisper, hand raised to his mouth as if masking the comment from the object of his disdain.

"I believe what I can see," Shane said. "Show me a ghost, and I'll believe in it."

"At that point, sometimes it's too late," Jasper said, tapping his nose with his forefinger as he drifted off.

"So you're the token skeptic?" Abby asked.

"Someone has to rein these people in," Shane smiled. "Otherwise, they'll convince themselves — with the best of intentions — that the ghost of Bigfoot is the one piloting all those UFOs."

"My mom saw a UFO once," one of the college girls said without looking up from her phone.

$$\text{———— } \boldsymbol{3}$$

She held her breath when they made love, she realized. Had she always? Fortunately, despite his braggadocio, it was over quickly, and she immediately fled to the bathroom, where she dry-heaved into the toilet.

It was *wrong*. She didn't know why, but that's how she felt now. Every single time.

"Jesus fucking Christ. Is this gonna happen every time?" Robert asked from the other room, not kindly.

"I'm sorry," she managed. She spit into the toilet. "I think... I think I might be pregnant." A lie, meant to placate him.

"You better be," he grumbled.

Five minutes later he was snoring.

Roberta slipped quietly out of the bathroom and drifted to the bedroom window. The only house she could see clearly was Abby's, directly across the street. Despite the streetlights, everything else not obscured by the gnarled trees groping skyward from the two center islands was swallowed up by darkness. She glanced at the digital clock on the bedside table. 12:23. Did she have to be up tomorrow? Did Robert? She couldn't remember. What a life. She couldn't stomach making love to her husband, and she didn't even know what day it was.

Motion, on the street outside. The big road, not the cul-de-sac.

She pressed her forehead against the glass and squinted for a better look.

Someone was coming, from the direction of the highway, but it wasn't a vehicle. On foot.

Several someones. Hard to see. They wore dark clothing. Flashes of white.

Kids? Vandals? She almost turned and reached for the bedside phone, but then her brain registered what she was seeing.

Adults. Six adult males in dark suits. The white she saw – white dress shirts, peeping out from behind dark grey or black jackets. And were they wearing sunglasses? In the middle of the night? A snatch of that song flitted through her brain.

They were carrying something, awkwardly, between them, three to the side. A crate?

They reached the circle of light thrown by the second streetlight from the corner and she gasped.

It was a coffin, the wood so smooth and black that the light skittered down one of its surfaces like it was the facet of a diamond.

My God, she thought. What are they doing? Where are they going?

It must be a cult, she reasoned. Some goofy bullshit ceremony, and they were doing it out here because this development

had been deserted for years

was new, so new that likely they didn't even know people lived here yet.

But they had to see the lights, right? Abby's porch light was on, and likely there were more on down the street. Those college girls at the far end were up all hours.

Maybe they just didn't care.

Whatever they were doing couldn't be *too* illegal then. Maybe not illegal at all.

So she continued to watch, fascinated.

The strange procession reached the corner and then *turned into their street.*

Holy shit, what the...?

They stopped. In front of her house.

She was shaking, she realized, clutching the curtains so hard with her right hand that she heard them tear, her other hand in her mouth. She always bit her fingers when she was nervous or scared, bit them bloody, sometimes.

Why was she so terrified? They were just people. Weirdos, clearly, but just people. They certainly had no interest in her.

And anyway, didn't Robert have a gun around here someplace? She'd wake him. She'd...

As one, all six heads turned in her direction.

The men were staring at her, through the window.

She gasped.

Then they turned, and began carrying their burden up her drive.

She screamed, long and loud, and her eyes popped open and she was in bed, soaked with sweat, and was it really just a dream was all that *really* just some crazy dream??? Robert shifted in his sleep beside her, his presence and physicality grounding her. It was a dream. Just some cray-cray dream.

Still, maybe she should slip out of bed and check the street... just to be sure?

No way, she decided. No way in hell.

——— *4*

There were, indeed, thirteen of them when the dust cleared and the various people aiding and assisting and responding to complaints and serving summonses and hanging around to say goodbye to a friend or family member finally dispersed. They still made for quite the caravan though – eight people crammed into the RV Professor Mahmoud had rented, Shane Whiteshroud driving the big, silver box truck, and the remainder following in their own vehicles. The site was seven hours away. After five, they made a pit stop at an unremarkable Denny's wannabe.

"Pretend we're three separate groups," insisted the professor. "If they seat more than five to a table, they tack on a mandatory gratuity."

Fucking cheapskate, thought Abby, who'd waited tables herself, when she was working her way through college.

She ended up sitting with Shane and two of the undergrad assistants. Jasper, who'd brought his dog – an irritating little yipper named "Patches" – opted to take the animal for a walk in lieu of eating, Winter Allegheny and Rachel-Megan DeVries never even left the RV.

"Hannah," one of the assistants introduced herself. The other one was Madison. "They've been referring to us as 'Daphne and Velma'. They think we don't know, but we do."

"They call the other assistant 'Buffy'," Madison added. "Her real name's Emily." She pointed Emily out to Abby. All three assistants were young and very, very pretty. And they consisted of one brunette, one blonde, and one redhead. *All three flavors of white girl*, as a tactless co-worker of hers once put it.

"I'm sure it's all in good fun," Shane said as he studied the menu.

"Well we're not here on a lark," Hannah frowned. "And we're bound to get all the shit details. A little respect would be nice."

"I'm not seeing any... male assistants," Abby ventured.

"That's 'cause Professor M is your classic dirty old perv," Madison said.

"Really?" This got Abby's hackles up. She'd dealt with similar nonsense throughout her career.

"He's not that old," Shane said.

Typical male reaction. Downplay it, turn it into a joke.

"You know," Hannah said, changing subjects, "Jasper specifically brought his dog along so that we'd be, like, thirteen-and-a-half or something. He called his 'life partner' in a panic and the guy rushed it over. He was pretty freaked that you'd made us thirteen."

"Well, originally I was just going to do some interviews before you set out, but then my boss thought it'd be keen if I tagged along." Abby looked to the trailer in the parking lot. "Truth, I was really angling for a sit-down with Rachel DeVries, and I haven't even seen her yet."

"Our 'celebrity'," Shane frowned.

"What's her deal, anyway?" Hannah asked, keeping her voice low. "I heard she got raped by a ghost."

"Jesus, Hannah," Madison said.

"She's not wrong," Abby said. "Rachel-Megan DeVries – she just goes by Rachel now – made the religious talk-show rounds a few months back, claiming that demons were inarguably real and she knew this because one had raped her before killing several of her friends."

"It was a house fire," Shane interjected. "I know the case."

"A house fire *set* by a demon," Abby corrected him. "At least, that's her story. She was a bit of a *cause célèbre* for the fundamentalist loony set for a few weeks, but then, all of a sudden, she dropped out of sight and refused to make any more public statements on the subject."

"It makes for good copy, I suppose."

"Absolutely," agreed Abby. "Rape, fire, demons, murder – all the good stuff."

The waitress was hovering, they realized, a look of distaste on her face.

"Do you have a vegan option?" Shane asked.

—— *5*

Emily – she was the blonde – rolled over and fell to the floor. Because she'd passed out on the couch, not in her bed. Hair sticking to her face, in her mouth, she climbed to her feet, using the coffee table for support. The living room was a disaster – beer bottles everywhere, stuff knocked over. She realized, belatedly, that she was in her t-shirt and panties. She wore a single sock.

"Ugh," she grunted. That said it all.

"Good morning, slutshine!" chirped Madison as she bounded out of the kitchen, Eggo waffle in hand, purse over her shoulder. Her long, chestnut hair was pulled back in a ponytail, and she had nice clothes on.

"How is it," Emily asked, sinking back into the sanctity of the couch, "you never have a hangover?"

"Just lucky, I guess."

"I don't even remember who was here last

night."

Madison riffled her brain. Damned if she couldn't remember either.

"Some... guys. And that bitch." The bitch she referred to was herself. Her little joke.

"I didn't do anything stupid, did I?" Emily's eyes were imploring her.

"Nope. You didn't start taking your clothes off until everybody left. You said it was too hot in here." A safe guess. Emily was always too hot.

"Thank God. Where are you off to, anyway?"

Madison froze. She didn't know.

"Errands," she said, finally. "Errands. Do you need anything?"

"Aspirin," Emily groaned.

——— *6*

"Wow," Abby said.

The seven identical houses were arranged around a sizable cul-de-sac, the view of those at the far end partially obscured by the dead trees thrusting out of a pair of center islands. Aside from the access road that brought them here, there was nothing else, for miles. Just a scrubby, patchy wasteland, dominated by yellowed, knee-high grass. The "lawns" in front of the houses were dirt.

"Why *two* center islands?" Abby asked. She was finally getting some face time with Professor Mahmoud while the others unloaded the van and the RV. He'd insisted she call him Ahmad.

"Three, actually. See the little triangular one there?" He pointed it out. "From the air, they look like two eyes and a nose. A skull."

"He really was committed to the gimmick, wasn't he?" Abby said, rolling her eyes.

"Ultimately, he was," Ahmad said. "Committed, I mean. But he got this far before the investors realized what he was doing with their money. When they fired him, he holed up in one of the units and had a sixteen-hour stand-off with police. Claimed he had a gun, but when they realized he was bluffing they barged in and dragged him out without further incident. It was that one," he pointed, "second on the right. Tried him and ultimately put him in the nut farm."

"They all really do look like *the* house," Abby went on, amazed. "Did you ever read the book?" she asked Ahmad.

"I saw the movie."

"Why?"

"I think I had free HBO that weekend."

"No, I mean why did he build this? How did it all come about?"

"Turn on your tape recorder," Ahmad said. "I'll give you your backstory."

"It's an app," she explained, pulling it up on her phone and tapping REC.

"So," Ahmad began, slipping into lecture mode, "as you may or may not know, Amityville, New York, is one of the most haunted places in America, possibly the world. The reasons for that are myriad and I won't go into them all, but there is a very real belief amongst many investigators that the entire village is situated smack dab on top of a portal to Hell. The literal Hell, with a capital H."

Abby nodded.

"Well in 2014 an architect named Stephen Madoff – no relation to Bernie – moved his family into one of several residences in Amityville known to be a focal point for intense psychic phenomenon. In short order they were besieged by apparitions and poltergeist activity, a veritable checklist of haunted house standards. They tried everything – ignoring it, living with it, bringing in people to bless the house and burn sage, so on and so forth. Finally, they threw in the towel. He sent the wife and kids to stay with a relative while he made arrangements to sell the place, at a loss. Pretty familiar story."

"It's literally every episode of *A Haunting*," Abby interjected.

"Exactly. Except this time, something different happened. Whether Stephen Madoff was possessed or just obsessed we'll never know, but over the next several weeks, while alone in that house, he came up with the idea to erect an entire row of homes that were exact duplicates of it, right down to the handles on the cabinet doors and the brand of light bulbs screwed into the sockets. And he did it. He screwed over a lot of people to make it happen, but he did it.

"And now, we believe that all of these houses are haunted too."

"That's quite a story." Abby stopped recording.

"It makes for good copy," Shane grinned, joining them.

"How's it looking?" Ahmad asked him.

"Good, good. For now we're setting all the

equipment up in one house, then we'll move it around as needed."

"How do they look inside?"

"Okay. We're much too far off the beaten path for vandals. They're all stage-furnished, so we can spread out if we like. No electricity, of course, and no water, but the porta-johns will be here by tonight and I'm heading into town to get supplies now, so we'll have plenty of drinking water."

Abby examined her phone and frowned.

"No bars," she said.

"Of course not," Ahmad laughed. "It wouldn't be a proper ghost story if you could call for help!"

$$\underline{\qquad}\ 7$$

"When are we going to get phone service out here?" Hannah asked. Dead receiver in hand, she stabbed the buttons on the kitchen wall phone for effect. "*Any* phone service?"

"I think it's kind of nice," Ahmad said, sipping his morning coffee. "Peaceful."

"You would. You're old."

"Old enough to want a newspaper to read with this coffee." He drummed his fingers on their tiny, dedicated breakfast table. There was a plate of scrambled eggs in front of him, barely touched. "I should start buying one on the way home from campus. I could read it the next morning and only be one day behind on the news."

"You're hopeless," the redhead said, draping her arms around his neck and kissing his cheek.

"You have any classes today?" he asked. "You can ride in with."

"Naw. I'm just gonna lounge around the house, read a book. Maybe I'll visit Em and Maddie next door."

"Those girls are trouble," Ahmad frowned.

"You're not my dad."

"I'm old enough to be your dad."

"Don't remind me," she laughed.

Ten minutes later, she waved from the window as he pulled out of the driveway.

Then she shuddered.

What in God's glorious fuck was she doing?

She drifted through the house, into "their" bedroom. Her clothes hung in the closet. Cherished belongings were neatly scattered about. Her little mongoose statuette. The framed picture with her parents at Yellowstone. Her baffled face stared back at her from the mirror over the dresser, her long, curly red hair gone now, chopped boy-short, which she vaguely remembered having done to make Ahmad find her less appealing. It suited her, unfortunately, and so her plan hadn't worked.

I'm *living* here.

How did this happen?

It wasn't a rhetorical question, asked by someone trying to determine the point at which their life had gone off the rails.

She honestly didn't know, couldn't remember.

When and why had she moved in with her psychology professor?

$$—— 8$$

"Hauling all that equipment from place to place?" the handsome black man said, shaking his head. "Total waste of effort." He held his phone so that she could see the screen and follow what he was doing. "I got everything you need, right here. EMF meter. EVP. Thermometer. Night vision. Infrasound. All apps."

"Impressive," said Abby.

"To you, and me, because we're smart. When Joe Sixpack thinks he's got a ghost, though, he's not so impressed with a brother strolling through the house, staring at his cell phone. He wants to see white folks waving all sorts of hardware around, beeping and covered with flashing lights. He wants the Ghostbusters."

"There was a black Ghostbuster," Abby reminded him. "Both times."

"Yeah, and both times they were the only *uneducated* Ghostbuster." Lionel shook his head.

"The struggle is real."

"Amen."

"So I know what an EMF meter is," Abby said. "And EVP is Electronic Voice Phenomenon – ghostly voices caught on tape. But what's infrasound?"

"Infrasound," Lionel explained, "is any sound less than 20 hertz per second. It's too low for human beings to consciously perceive, but we can *feel* it. It makes us nervous, agitated, feel like we're being watched. Sometimes it messes with your head so much you start to see things. It's often caused by something metallic vibrating at *just* the right frequency. If I'm picking up a lot of infrasound, you don't have ghosts, you've got a poorly-mounted AC unit or issues with your pipes."

"So those two plumbers from *Ghost Hunters* might come in handy after all."

"First time for everything," Lionel laughed.

"Not a fan, I take it?"

"Those fu-... Excuse me. Those *clowns*, all the theatrical amateurs inspired by them, and skeptics like our Mr. Whiteshroud," he nodded in the Indian's direction, "are two sides of the same coin. They cheapen the entire discipline. It's like they're working from opposite ends to turn a legitimate branch of science into a spook-show joke."

"So you absolutely believe in ghosts."

"I believe that 99% of ghosts are infrasound, tricks of the light, misidentifications, and straight

up baloney."
    "And the other one percent?"
    He grinned.
    "That's why we're here."

———— **9**

"Oh, Patches, what *is* your malfunction?" Jaspar sighed as he hung up the dog's leash.

For the umpteenth time, the little dog had positioned itself in front of the floor-level cabinet in the corner of the kitchen – the one next to the ice maker – and refused to budge, ears back, hair bristling, a low rumble rattling in the back of its throat.

"What do you think is in there, hmm? A raccoon? You're much too small to tussle with a raccoon, you know. Even a squirrel should give *you* pause."

The dog responded with a low, plaintive whine.

"Your treats aren't in there either, you know, so I don't know what you're trying to prove. Come into the living room with me and we'll have a little snack and watch our *SportsCenter*."

Reluctantly, the dog tore itself away and

followed its master into the living room.

Every day with this nonsense, Jasper thought. Not for the first time, he wondered what got Patches so riled up about that specific cabinet.

Likely, it would forever remain a mystery. Because, truth be told, Jasper was afraid to open it.

———— *10*

"Abilene Beaumont. Who saddled a lovely lady like you with a mouthful like that?"

"Born in one, conceived in the other, or so I'm told."

"Really?" Robert said. He'd asked her to call him Rob.

"That's the story. It's actually my first and middle name, but I adopted it as my byline because *Abby Smith* just sounded so... beige."

"We can sympathize," said Roberta. Bobbi. Abby was watching as they calibrated their equipment. It was all standard ghost hunting gear; the pair ran a tiny paranormal investigation company out of Jacksonville, and were the most stereotypical of the investigators invited to this party. They were also the most eager. While everyone else concentrated on setting up a nerve center, they'd decided to do a little preliminary exploring, and Abby had invited herself along.

She guessed that it would be far more interesting than watching Ahmad and the Japanese fellow argue about where to set up the generator, and her primary quarry was still hiding out in the RV.

"I mean, *Robert* and *Roberta*?" Bobbi went on. "I have no idea what our parents were thinking."

"Just once," said her brother, "I'd like to meet identical twins whose names aren't alliterative or rhyming."

"Seriously," said Bobbi. "What's wrong with naming twin boys, say, Richard and Todd? Is that really so outré? Would society crumble?"

"So tell me about your methodology," Abby said. "What's the first thing professional psychical researchers do when they're approached to investigate a potential haunting?"

"Well, first," Rob said, "we like to call ourselves *physical* researchers, not psychical, because we demand actual, physical evidence."

"Also, *psychical* is a dumb, redundantal word that's hard to say," Bobbi chimed in.

"So the first thing we do," Rob continued, "is make sure our equipment is in proper working order. The most important piece of equipment, of course, being the camera." He held the digital videocam up for emphasis. "No point in detecting anything if we can't prove it to the skeptics later."

"Not that they'll accept much of anything *as* proof," Bobbi said. "I swear, a ghost could fly up that Shane Whiteshroud's ass and do the Batusi and he'd blame it on something he ate for lunch."

"So you know each other?" Abby asked.

"Oh, we know each other." Bobbi didn't hide her irritation.

"He used to show up at our investigations," Rob explained. "Just barge in and start spouting off about how our methods were a bunch of hogwash and that we weren't there to help, just to collect evidence to support our 'cockamamie theories'. He got arrested for trespassing, once."

"He seems so low-key," Abby frowned. "He's been really nice. To me, anyway."

"Of course," said Bobbi. "He's in enemy territory. He's looking for allies."

"Okay," Rob said, hefting the videocam dramatically into the air, like it was a handgun. "Let's go find some ghosts!"

———— *11*

Winter poked her head out the front door. The gay man had walked his little dog, everyone who was going to "work" had left, and even one of the college girls had driven off somewhere. She wondered, briefly, where the ones with "jobs" went all day. They didn't really have jobs, of course. They couldn't possibly. **They** would never allow...

She immediately banished the thought, buried it beneath a screen of distressing memories that she kept on tap, to be instantly dredged up for this very purpose. Her grandmother's funeral. The first time she'd seen a dead animal. That song from the cartoon movie about rabbits, the one that always made her cry.

She had to be careful. If It even suspected...

"Winter?" Suki, her "husband", calling from somewhere upstairs.

"Out front," she answered, stepping outside.

"I'm going for a walk," she called back, and set out without waiting for a response. Already, just putting some distance between herself and that house, the dank, omnipresent oppression seemed to fall away. Not entirely, of course, but to such a degree that she felt as if she could simply lift her arms and take flight, far, far away from this horrible place.

She circled the cul-de-sac twice, enjoying the fresh air, oblivious to the semi-distant sounds of construction. A nudge too skinny, she certainly didn't need the exercise, but she didn't want to make any of Them suspicious. So she ambled, lingered, paused in front of some of Them, pretending to wonder if anyone was home. Then, after her second cycle, just before she reached Lionel's house at the very head of the circle, she suddenly veered right, through his yard, and came out behind it in an endless field of tall grass, reportedly swarming with fruit rats and the rattlesnakes that fed on them. She'd never seen evidence of either. Here, the air tasted cleaner somehow, and she inhaled deeply, filling her lungs. As usual she wore black – a plain black t-shirt and tight black jeans – and these eagerly soaked up the sun, easing the chill that she always felt while in the neighborhood proper.

Someone whistled at her. A wolf whistle.

A laborer, next street over. An identical cul, with seven identical houses going up. She shuddered.

"Lookin' good, Freak Show!" the laborer called

out, thrusting his pelvis at her suggestively. She'd encountered him before. Or maybe not. They were all the same, literally. There was no point in flipping him the bird, but she did so anyway, and then turned right and walked on, deeper into the fields, further from the houses and the construction.

When she reached the RV five minutes later, she was distressed to see that one of the tires had gone entirely flat. She couldn't quite say why this bothered her so much. A premonition, perhaps. She rapped on the door with a single knuckle.

"Entré."

Winter opened the door and stepped inside. The trailer was dark, the windows clumsily plastered with copy paper to keep out the sun, and reeked of incense. An open can of pears, empty, sat on the kitchenette table, a spoon sticking out of it. The lid was jagged, like it had been cut open with a knife. Rachel, naked, was sprawled out on the bed in the rear, but sat up when Winter entered. Winter felt a brief pang of jealously. With her hair hanging in her face, masking the scarring, Rachel was one of the prettiest things she had ever seen.

"Hey there, silver hair," Rachel said, in the cadence of the supremely stoned. "You bring me anything?"

Winter shook her head. "Tonight, if you need it. I just had to get away."

Rachel fell back into the bed.

"I don't know why you stick around this

place," she said. "This death hole. This shit-hell."

"I have to. I have to put a stake in all this. I have to... do something."

"So do it."

"You wouldn't try to stop me?" Winter asked.

Rachel cackled. She sounded unhinged.

"Stop you? Why forever would I stop you, Romeo? My silver-tressed Romeo?"

"It's just... I don't want to assume where your loyalties lie. Your... needs."

"My needs?" the naked girl said, incredulous. "I'm barren, dead inside. Finished. It might as well have filed my clitoris off. There's nothing left. Nothing.

"YOU BASTARD!" she shrieked, an agonizing blend of grief and loss and white-hot hate.

Jesus, Winter thought. Time to bounce.

"*Oh God, oh God, oh Satan...*" Rachel sobbed, rolling over and burying her face in her pillow.

"I'll bring you some things tonight," Winter promised, slipping out the door.

12

The first house on the right, as you pulled in, is where everything was being unloaded, so that left six other houses for them to explore. "Got a preference?" Rob asked.

"That one," said his sister, pointing. "The second one in. That's where Madoff had his stand-off with the police. Might be some lingering energy there."

"This is going to be an interesting investigation," Rob explained to Abby as the trio strolled to the next house. "No one's ever lived – or died – in these houses, so there shouldn't be any residual energy at all. Whatever's here is something inherent in the structures themselves."

"What makes you think something *is* here?" Abby asked.

"Madoff had a plan," Bobbi said. "What it was, we don't know. But that house – the original house – took control of him and *compelled* him to do this. It must have had a reason."

"They say," Rob added as they reached the front stoop, "that he stripped elements from the original house and incorporated them into all of these. A length of pipe here, a light switch plate there. He thought this would... transfer the activity."

"Like a computer virus," Abby said,

"Exactly."

They paused on the stoop.

"Door's unlocked," Rob said. "Would anyone like to do the honors?"

Abby stepped up and opened the front door.

It swung smoothly on like-new hinges. A hallway, stairs, parallel, leading to the second floor. A largish living room, complete with fireplace, opened off to the right. At the other end of the hallway would be the kitchen, a half bath, and the dining room, the latter of which could also be accessed through the living room. Even with light creeping in through the curtainless windows it was dark, darker, it seemed, than it should be. There was a weighty, conflicting mixture of new construction and stale in the air.

"Most of the phenomenon in the original house took place upstairs and in the basement," Rob continued, "but Madoff was forced to forgo the basements because the water table here is too high."

"What's a 'basement'?" joked Bobbi. The twins were Florida natives.

"Upstairs, then?" Abby asked. Bobbi was already sweeping the hallway with her EMF meter. Rob was filming her.

"Actually," Bobbi said, "I'd like to check out the living room. That's where Stephen Madoff communicated with police by shouting through a broken window."

They stepped through the archway into the living room. Fireplace. Staging furniture – a sofa, an end table, and two club chairs. A large, framed landscape broke up the monotony of the longest wall. The windows to the right looked out on the street and one of them was, indeed, broken. Slowly, Bobbi swept the meter in her hand to the left, then the right, up, then down.

Rob nodded. "Tell the camera what you're doing," he said.

"So this is an EMF meter," Bobbi explained, favoring the camera with an infectious smile. "It detects electromagnetic fields. Since ghosts are essentially disembodied energy, this is one of the best ways to detect their presence. I... wait..." She smiled again. "Off the charts!" she said, turning the meter to the camera.

Indeed, the needle was redlining. Then, after wavering for a moment, it dropped to nothing.

"Could this furtive entity be mad architect Stephen Madoff's ghost?" Rob suggested, for the camera.

"Madoff didn't die here," Abby reminded them. "According to Professor Mahmoud he isn't even dead."

Bobbi shot Abby a dirty look.

"Shh!" Rob hissed.

"Again, from the top," Bobbi said.

They reenacted the entire scene, sans the part where Bobbi turned the meter to the camera.

"I'll cut the reading in later," Rob said.

"Is there anything else that might set one of those things off?" Abby asked when they were finished. "I mean, what's an EMF meter actually for?"

"Like I said," Bobbi repeated, "it detects electromagnetic fields."

"Wouldn't that have an electromagnetic field?" Abby asked, pointing to the bare light bulb screwed into a socket jutting from the ceiling.

"Well, yes, normally. But these houses don't have any power." Bobbi flipped the light switch on the wall behind her for emphasis.

The light came on. Blindingly bright, it flooded the room with harsh, contrasting white. Everyone instinctively shut their eyes, only to find themselves staring at a harsh green afterimage in the shape of a light bulb. Then, almost immediately, the light began to fade.

"Get that! Get that!" Bobbi shouted. Rob swung the camera on the bulb and managed to frame it just before it winked out.

"Holy shit!" Bobbi said. She was giddy. "That was amazing!"

"Maybe it was just some leftover electricity in the system?" Abby stared at the naked bulb, perplexed.

"Electricity doesn't work like that," Rob said. "That there was a legitimate paranormal experience!"

"Welcome to the mutherfuckin' ghost 'hood!" Bobbi said.

———— _13_

Machinery slumbering, workmen vanished, the access road was eerily dark and quiet as Abby drove home. She thought, probably not for the first time, that they really needed to erect some streetlights before someone drifted off the road and crashed into an off-duty bulldozer.

Hanging left into the cul, she went the wrong way so that she could immediately turn into her drive, the first on the left. She was the only one who could do this with any degree of safety; the foliage on the center islands limited visibility beyond the two lots nearest the corner. But she didn't think about that now. She'd seen something, something that hadn't been there before. Sliding out of the car, she strode to the corner, where the gleaming object jutted out of the earth, straight and true.

A street sign. Her street sign. They'd finally put it up, and since the cul _did_ have streetlights, she could easily read it.

"Apprehension".

What the hell? That wasn't the name of the street! It was...

Was...

She couldn't remember.

What was wrong with her? She couldn't remember anything anymore; dates, times, whole swathes of her day seemed to crumble into a murky haze the moment she got home. Was it early-onset Alzheimer's or something? Suddenly she needed a cigarette, even though she hadn't smoked since college, and barely then, to be honest.

She'd dig out an old piece of mail. The street's proper name would be printed there.

Of course, she couldn't remember the last time she got any mail. There had to be something though, an electric bill, something. She marched back to the house, let herself in, and tried to recall where she usually put the unopened mail. Back in her apartment she'd always tossed it on the little hall table...

Apartment.

When did...

The little hall table was there. With the drawer and the big chip in the side where Barry had...

She felt a migraine coming on.

There was no mail, unopened or otherwise, on the table. But there was a pack of smokes. She didn't remember buying them, but she was glad to see them now.

She found a grill lighter in the kitchen and turned to go back outside. Then she had a better idea. Climbing the stairs, she stepped out on the second floor balcony. The center islands' trees still blocked much of her view of the neighborhood proper, but she could see a fair distance in every other direction, even in the dark. She lit her cigarette, took a long drag, and tried to get her shit together.

How long had she lived here, again? She wracked her brain.

She couldn't remember. Not just how long. Any of it. Making the decision. Packing. Unpacking. Signing the lease or loan paperwork or whatever...

And... where was Princess Whiskers!?

She was instantly flooded with adrenaline. And clarity. She *never* would have relocated without her beloved kitty! Where was she??? Did...

She exhaled, the smoke traveling only a few inches from her lips before rolling around something, giving it form, something right in front of her that she couldn't otherwise see.

A face.

She screamed, stumbled backwards.

It was already gone, the smoke that had outlined it dissipating into the night air.

A trick of the light? It must have been. A trick of the...

She felt its solidity pressing against her leg, screamed and backpedaled again.

"Mereow?" She could almost hear the cat questioning her sanity.

Jesus Christ.

"How long have you been locked out here?" she asked Princess Whiskers. Scooping the cat up, she carried it inside. "I need a hot bath," she declared. "And at least half a bottle of Pinot." Princess Whiskers watched impassively as Abby gathered up her paraphernalia and made for the upstairs bathroom. As soon as she was out of sight, the cat faded away as if it had never existed.

Light stands had been set up in a large circle, portable grills and coolers had been pulled out of trunks, a plastic garbage bin was already filling up with dead soldiers and party debris. Jasper's little dog ran from one person to the next, earning scraps and making friends. It looked less like a scientific excursion than a tailgating party. Someone tossed Rob a beer, putting a serious spin on it, but he sidestepped and let it land in the street, where it burst open and spun off across the concrete, a trail of foam in its wake. "Watch the camera!" he snapped.

"What in the world...?" Abby asked.

"There you are!" Ahmad said, arms wide, a huge smile on his face. He was obviously a few beers deep. "The gang's all here!"

"What's going on?" Bobbi asked.

"Our nerve center is assembled and fully operational, generator's running smoothly, supplies stocked. So I figured we should all let off a little steam before we get down to business. And it's a chance for everyone who hasn't met yet to get to know each other!"

At this Abby looked around and quickly found her. Rachel-Megan DeVries. Loose t-shirt. Jeans. Practical boots. Hair an unkempt tangle. Even with the massive scarring on the left side of her face – from the fire – she was attractive, but she was clearly playing down her looks. Apart from the others, she leaned against the RV, sipping what Abby first took to be a beer but which turned out to be a can of Cheerwine.

"Where have you all been, anyway?" Ahmad asked, slipping his arm around Bobbi's shoulder. It was meant to be friendly, probably, but it came across as skeevy, like he just wanted an excuse to touch her.

"We were doing a little prelim. Just poking around." Rob shot Abby a look as he said this and she got the message: Don't mention the incident with the light bulb.

"For three hours?" Ahmad asked. "Sounds to me like you were just trying to get out of helping set up!"

Three hours? Only now did it dawn on Abby that it was dusk, and late dusk at that, the powerful lights mounted to the stands barely keeping the darkness at bay. How had that little excursion taken them three hours?

"Everyone, our prodigals have returned!" Ahmad announced, raising his hands and freeing

Bobbi, who immediately scampered out of reach. "For those who don't know," he continued, "the smiling pair that look like Donny and Marie Osmond..." Bobbi cringed at the comparison "...are Rob and Bobbi Remington, of the Jacksonville Paranormal Alliance, or JAP." He pronounced it *Jap*, so now it was Suki Kobayashi's turn to cringe, and Abby, a stickler for language and usage, joined him, because *Jackson Paranormal Alliance* should obviously be abbreviated *JPA*, not *JAP*.

"You all know me, of course," the professor continued. "Investigator Lionel Holland is handling grill duties..." Lionel raised his spatula "...that's our tech guy and resident physicist Mr. Kobayashi fiddling with the lights, psychics Jasper Janowitz and Winter Allegheny are the duo over there, hopefully comparing impressions, this is our unofficial chronicler Abilene Beaumont..." he indicated Abby "... and last but hardly least, our undergrad assistants Madison, Hannah, and Emily." The three young girls, who were clustered together, all cheered and raised the beers in their hands. They were openly drunk.

"Oh, and Shane Whiteshroud," Ahmad concluded, "obligatory skeptic, on drums." Shane's eyes narrowed. He clearly didn't appreciate Ahmad's little jibe.

The professor hadn't mentioned Rachel DeVries at all, Abby noted.

But there she was, nonetheless, furtively

disengaged from the action, sipping her sugary soda.

To approach or not to approach, that was the question.

"Excuse me," she said to no one in particular, making her decision. Rachel locked eyes with her as she approached, then continued to stare silently when they were finally face to face. The laughter, the conversation, the innumerable sounds that accompany people gathered together, all seemed to fade into the background, muffled, inconsequential.

"You're the reporter," Rachel said.

"Don't worry," Abby smiled, extending her hand. "I'm not going to..."

"I'm not worried," Rachel cut her off.

They studied each other for a moment.

"Walk with me," Rachel said.

She strolled off, away from the group, and Abby followed.

They passed one house. Two. The darkness settled around them with a comforting weight, like swaddling clothes. Rachel stopped, sighed, stared up at the stars. Here, away from any significant light pollution, they were uncountable. Rachel drained the last of her soda and tossed the empty can into the nearest yard. Unsodded, the yards consisted entirely of dirt and unusually tenacious weeds.

"What do you want?" the girl asked, her back to Abby. "An interview? I was on *The Talk*. Why don't you just watch my appearance on *The Talk*?

Paraphrase it. Embellish it, if you want. I don't care."

"I wanted to meet you," Abby said carefully. "I wanted to..."

"What?" Rachel cut her off again. "Jettison the glad-handling preamble."

"Fine. I want to know why you're here. If you're really looking for answers or if it's all just a publicity stunt to benefit Professor Mahmoud's spook busters dog and pony show. I want to know," she took a deep breath, "if you really believe."

"Believe," Rachel repeated.

"Yes."

"You want to know what I believe. What I really believe?"

"Yes."

Rachel's answer was emotionless, matter-of-fact.

"I believe there's an unnatural presence here. And I'm going to fuck it."

————— *15*

The television was an ancient, cabinet-style job, heavy as guilt, which is why Jasper hated the nightly ritual of turning it around so that it faced the wall.

But it had to be done.

Ever since that night. How long ago had it been now? Three weeks, at least. He'd come downstairs, half asleep, craving a midnight snack. His eyes had wandered to the right as he passed the living room and...

And.

The dullest of glows from the TV screen, barely perceptible. It wasn't on, but it wasn't *not* on, either. He'd stopped, stared at it, shook his head to clear the sleep and ensure that he wasn't half dreaming. His first thought was that maybe the screen always looked like that in the dark, whether because it was plugged in and had *some* power surging through it, or perhaps due to a reflection from outside.

But no, it was neither of those things. Because there was something *moving* behind the screen. Chest tight, he'd moved closer.

Faces, pressed against the screen.

And, dear God, they could *see* him.

They *reacted* as he approached, a mixture of excitement and envy and something darker, simmering just below the surface.

He'd backed up slowly, out of the room, the faces silently bemoaning his departure, their eyes following him until he was out of sight. Only when he was in the hallway again had he realized that he'd pissed himself in terror. The next thing he knew he was upstairs, in the shower, and then in bed, covers over his head, a quizzical Patches held tight in his arms. The next morning he almost convinced himself that he'd imagined it.

Almost.

He never saw the faces again. Benign by the light of day, or while a show was on, it was only at night, when the set was turned off, that he sensed them there, eager, grasping.

But at those times, now, the television was always turned towards the wall.

—————— *16*

Ten minutes later Abby walked slowly back towards the circle of light and noise and normalcy, then, at the last moment, veered left and plopped down in the front yard of the first house on the right, the Nerve Center. They'd have to name the houses, or number them, or something, she thought absently. There were no posted addresses.

A shape detached itself from the surrounding darkness, approached her, squatted down.

"Join you?" asked Lionel.

"Sure."

He sat down, made himself comfortable amongst the dirt and weeds, sipped the beer in his hand.

"Saw you wander off with Ms. DeVries," he said eventually. "Enlightening, or frightening?"

"A little of both. Mostly the latter." She turned to him, her face an unreadable mixture of confusion and sympathy and just a little awe. "Great googly moogly, Lionel. I think she's crazy!"

"You don't smoke anymore, but right now you could really use a cigarette."

"I thought Jasper and Winter were the psychics."

"Not psychic. Just observant." He produced a pack of American Spirits and she took one. He lit it for her with a clear, pink disposable lighter.

"The shit she believes, I mean, my *God*..." She inhaled deeply, then slowly blew the smoke out through her teeth.

"I think most of this crew believes in some weird shit," Lionel said, lighting a cigarette himself. "Me included."

"So what's your story?" Abby asked. "What got you chasing ghosts?"

Lionel laughed.

"Define *ghost*," he said.

"C'mon."

"No, really. I don't believe in ghosts. At least, I don't believe they're the souls of dead people come back to hassle us. Heck, I'm not even sure I believe in God. I mean, a magic spirit that lives in outer space and grants our wishes, but only sometimes? That's a lot to swallow."

"My Wednesday School teacher would have a categorical answer for that, I'm sure."

"Wednesday School?"

"Our services tended to run over, so they held Sunday School on Wednesday."

"Ah."

"So what do you believe?" Abby asked. She absently drew a circle in the dirt with her finger, then put a slash through it.

"Glad you asked," Lionel smiled. His smile was catching, and she smiled back. "Wanna hear my story?"

"Sure."

"Okay, well it's a funny thing, because this incident, when it happened, was just a thing that happened, you know? I didn't make much of it, not until later." Leaning back on one elbow, he settled in and so did Abby. "I was a freshman in college. Now, the school I went to, all freshmen were required to live in the dorms for the first year, with a roommate. It was mandatory – a life lesson kind of thing. Teaching kids who'd never lived with anyone besides their parents and maybe siblings how to deal with a roommate who was essentially a stranger, you know? Compromise, and all that. So, obviously, everyone who lived in this dorm was matched up with a roommate, two to a room. Nobody was allowed their own room. Nobody.

"Except Aasim.

"Aasim was the only one who had his own room. No roommate. This was completely against the rules. The weird thing is, the rest of us on the floor, we never really acknowledged it, or even thought anything of it. It was just the way things were.

"So one night, maybe two-thirds into the

semester, middle of the night, there's all this ruckus in the hallway. So my roomie and I – everyone on the floor, really – all pour out into the hallway and here's this strange kid just flipping his lid, screaming at Aasim, claiming he's Aasim's roommate and where was all his stuff. He sounded, well, crazy, but not mental crazy; more like, that kind of panicked crazy where you've reached the end of your tether and are full out of options.

"So he's hollering at Aasim, and then he turns on *us*, me and my roommate. Now, we've never seen this kid before in our lives, but he just goes off, insisting that we know him and we've known him since the semester began and why are we doing this to him, why are we helping Aasim fuck with him.

"And the shit of it is, *he knows our names.* And not just the two of us, and Aasim, but everyone on the floor. First, last, facts about us. Like he's been there all along.

"So finally the floor monitor shows up and he tells this kid to fuck the fuck off or he's gonna call campus security. But the kid's all 'Go ahead! I have my student I.D.! It proves I live here!' Looking back, I wish he would've busted out that I.D., shown it to somebody. But he never got the chance because at that point the monitor got into a little scuffle with him. Not a fight, really, just some grabbing and pushing and finally the monitor's like 'Fuck this, I'm calling the cops!' and that's when this kid finally jets, down the fire stairs and out the back door, cussing all of us the whole way."

"So who was he?" Abby asked.

"Dunno. Security showed up about fifteen minutes later, and they scoured the campus looking for him, but he just disappeared. Like he was never there."

"Sounds like a prank to me," Abby said, frowning.

"Maybe. I mean, he could've gotten our names from the facebook, sure. But to what end? And how did he know all those little facts about us? He wasn't a student, at least as far as we could ever determine. And believe me, he was a major topic of interest for the next couple of weeks. We looked for him, hard. No one ever, ever saw him again."

"So you think he was a ghost?"

"In a way. I think he just kind of... slipped into the wrong reality. Like he came from a world where he *was* Aasim's roommate, our friend, a student at the university, always had been, and somehow he ended up, briefly, in a world where none of that was true. *That's* what I think ghosts are."

"People who have glitched into a different reality."

"Exactly." Lionel stubbed his cigarette out in the dirt. "One thing really bothers me though. And it is why I think this research is so important."

"What's that?"

"All those months when Aasim inexplicably had his own room. Maybe he *did* have a roommate. Maybe this kid glitched out of *our* reality, and then back in, but the universe corrected itself in the interim and we all just forgot him."

"Like he never existed," Abby said quietly. Lionel nodded.

"Like a ghost."

$$\text{———— } \textbf{\textit{17}}$$

Winter waited until she was sure Itsuki was asleep, then quietly slipped out of bed and down the stairs. Foregoing any inner monologue, striving to keep her mind an utter blank, she collected the bag of groceries she'd gathered earlier and walked out the front door, barefoot, in her nightgown, making a beeline for Lionel's house at the head of the cul, through his yard, and into the fields beyond. Her movements were rote, robotic, and only when the neighborhood proper was behind her, drenched in darkness, did she relax. Switching the bag to her other arm (it was heavy – mostly canned goods) she continued on, her step natural now, until she reached the RV. She rapped lightly on the door and let herself in without waiting for an answer.

"Rachel?" she stage whispered. She wiped the night damp from one bare foot with the other. She didn't want to track it in.

"Here," Rachel answered. The beam of a powerful flashlight, aimed at the ceiling, instantly illuminated the interior of the RV in dull grays, shadows fanning out in every direction. Winter placed the bag she'd brought on the kitchenette table.

"Canned green beans. Canned corn. Canned peaches. Soda. Tortilla chips. The chips are expired but only a couple of days."

"Diet soda or regular?" Rachel asked. The indirect light made a harsh, shadowy mask of her face.

"Diet."

"Pure cancer."

"Like regular soda doesn't give you cancer."

"Regular soda gives you diabetes. Diet soda gives you cancer. Is cancer."

"Suit yourself." Winter punctuated this by plucking a Diet Pepsi out of the bag, popping it, and taking a sip. It was warm and tasted like medicine.

"Stay with me?" Rachel asked.

"For a while. I should get back before Suki wakes up."

"It sees through him." Voicing the obvious.

"It sees through all of them." Extrapolating the obvious. She climbed into bed next to Rachel, held her. It wasn't sexual. Their need was far more basic, even, than that. "We should leave," she said, after a time. "Get away."

"No. It has to pay."

"I'll go without you."

"You won't. Your conscience won't let you. Someone has to stop it, here and now. And we can't just cast it out, you know. We're way past that. We have to demolish it, raze it, murder its children and salt the earth. You and Jasper, you're the only ones who can confront it on a higher plane. "

"Jasper's gone," Winter said quietly. "I see him, walking his dog. He doesn't know yet. He's still going through the motions."

"Then you definitely can't leave," Rachel said. "You're our only hope."

18

The lights were doused one by one and people were drifting away, either to camp out in the Nerve Center or sleep in the RV. Cots and bedrolls were produced, supplies stashed, trash collected and disposed of by the undergrad assistants, giggling and tipsy. The party ended with a whimper rather than a bang.

"I think I'm going to sleep outside," Bobbi said. "Under these amazing stars. Normally the bugs would drive me batty, but there don't seem to be any."

It was true. The night had been insect free.

"Kind of a letdown," Shane said, drifting over to where Abby and Rob now stood. "I figured you crazy pagan white folks would wrap this up by burning someone alive in a wicker goat."

"Maybe tomorrow," Rob said. He stared daggers at the Indian then quickly excused himself.

"They do not like you," Abby said.

"I'm a threat to their nonsense. And look at this mess." Shane indicted the litter left behind, despite the girls' halfhearted cleanup attempt. As if on cue, the wind plucked up a piece of paper debris and sent it wafting past, carrying it off into the night. "Wait for it. I'll shed a single tear."

Abby didn't get it, and admitted as much.

"Pop culture reference," he explained. "Before your time."

Soon, they were the only two left, aside from Rob, who'd collected a still camera and was strolling down the street, randomly taking pictures, and Bobbi, who had, indeed, set up her cot in the front yard of the Nerve Center and was staring up at the sky.

"What is he hoping to get a picture of?" Abby asked.

"Orbs," Shane said, shaking his head. The word dripped with disdain.

"The little balls of light, right?"

"Yeah. Just the flash reflecting off insects or dust or other tiny particles in the air."

"The skeptical answer," Abby smiled.

"The scientific answer," Shane corrected her. "That 'orb' effect generally occurs when a camera's flash is situated too close to its lens, and, big surprise, you never heard much about 'orbs' until the advent of digital cameras, which are really thin..."

"So that the flash is too close to the lens," Abby finished for him.

"I'll make a skeptic out of you yet," Shane grinned.

"You really don't believe there might be more out there?"

"There is more out there. So much more. Wonders undreamt of. Animals and plants and landscapes and things we can't even begin to imagine. That's why all *this* irks me. So many amazing things in the world – in the universe – so many things left to discover, and these people spend all their time chasing flights of fancy. And it's not because they want to illuminate or learn, no. It's all ego. They just can't admit that they were wrong."

"You're a very cynical man, Shane Whiteshroud."

"Cynicism is just realism, as perceived by the gullible. No offense."

"None taken. I've never seen myself as the gullible type."

"I saw you wander off with our celebrity earlier. Did you get your exclusive?"

"Oh my God," Abby rolled her eyes. "She's crazy."

"What did she have to say?"

"I mean, I'm not sure if she told me this in confidence or..."

"Don't say anything if you shouldn't."

"No, I want your take on this. As a skeptic." Abby took a deep breath. "Okay, so she claims she was, indeed, sexually assaulted by a... spirit. And of course it was a violation, and as horrible as anything like that could be, and she assured me that she didn't want to cheapen what other women had gone through. Not with spirits, of course..."

"Of course."

"*But*, she said, after it was all over, in retrospect, she realized that... that she'd *enjoyed* it."

"Enjoyed it?"

"Yes. And she wanted it to happen again. Only she wanted to be in the driver's seat this time."

"So our Ms. DeVries is here to – excuse me if this sounds flip – boff a ghost?"

"Essentially. Except she assured me that there aren't any 'ghosts' here. She believes this housing development was built to highly precise specifications in order to attract, well..." She shook her head.

"You trailed off dramatically there."

"Sorry. It's all so..." She looked away, feeling foolish and frightened and even more foolish for being so frightened. "She says that this place is Disneyland for demons."

INTERLUDE: NOW

Princess Whiskers wore out her welcome early in the third week, when she decided to chew on the covers of several semi-rare XTC records. She spent the entire next day and most of the following night in her Kitty Karry Kase, squalling, then the rest of the night in the bathroom, where she shredded several rolls of toilet paper and peed all over the floor. In the morning, Nancy stuffed her back into her carrying case and took her to Abby's sister's.

Which is when she learned that no one had heard from Abby since she'd left.

This wasn't *excessively* unusual. Abby had been out of contact, on assignment, for lengthy periods before. In truth, Nancy, swamped with work at the spa, had barely noticed that her BFF hadn't checked in. Nevertheless, something suddenly didn't sit right. A seed had been planted, and while Nancy was able to relegate it to the back of her mind, dismiss the subsequent phone calls that went straight to voicemail and remained unanswered for another week, then two, it was only a matter of time before her subconscious demanded she take notice.

It came, as it often does, in the form of a dream. As with many of her more lucid dreams, this one presented its dream-logic backstory as narration.

The Old Man saw a painting somewhere of a creepy old house perched on top of a skyscraper, and because he thought this was nifty and because he had the kind of money that allowed a man to do most anything, he made it happen. Not a new construct but an actual, pre-existing house, carefully disassembled and re-constituted at its new location in mid-town Manhattan, surrounded by walls of thick, clear plastic to keep the high-altitude winds from tearing it apart or carrying it over the side. But it was the house he selected that made this more than a New York Post *one-columner. You know the one – it was in all the papers and on television in its day. And they made those movies. In time most people forgot, of course, but not everybody. Not the Old Man, clearly.*

In the dream, Nancy had been invited to the house, to some sort of soiree, likely because she was young and reasonably attractive and the Old Man was a lech. There were celebrities there, and strange, scary-movie things kept happening that no one could explain. At one point, a well-known musician left the house in a preternatural daze, convinced that he was visiting a normal house in any given suburban neighborhood. He found his way outside the safety wall, strolled off the side of the building, and plunged sixty-six floors to his death. When she awoke, most of the narrative – such as it was – was a nonsensical blur, but Nancy remembered one thing clearly: the creepy old house had been *alive*, and this was important, somehow.

Hadn't Abby gone off to investigate some haunted house?

She had the dream again the next night, and the next, and when you dream something three nights in a row, that means it's true.

Abby was in trouble.

It took her two days to finagle the time off work, and another half day of phone calls and research to determine where this "haunted neighborhood" Abby was writing about was even located. Central Florida. A ten-hour drive. Okay.

She left at noon the next day.

The drive was uneventful, a parade of featureless highway and perfunctory fuel stops and soul-crushing gas station food. She wished, more than once, that she'd packed something healthy to eat. She made good time though, and it wasn't quite 8:30 PM when she found herself lost on what had to be the tail end of the final leg of her journey. A convenience store lurched out of the twilight and she pulled in. Big Guy Mart.

The man behind the counter gave her the *we're closing soon* glare. She grabbed a packet of something at random, just so she wouldn't be one of *those* customers when she told him "I'm kinda lost."

"Where ya headin'?" the man asked as he rang up her purchase. It was a bag of nuts, she realized. Appropriate.

"Well, I'm not sure how to describe it...." She struck a pose and cranked up the charm. Couldn't hurt. "I don't know the name. It's kind of a... ghost town, I guess?"

"Ghost town? Like some tourist horseshit or an actual, abandoned town?"

"Well, not a town, exactly. More like an abandoned housing development. But new. No one's ever lived there, I don't think."

Comprehension dawned as he made her change. Four bucks and change for a tiny bag of mixed nuts? Jesus.

"Bullshit Acres."

"Excuse me?" She grinned, hardly offended.

"That's what they call it. Out in the middle of nowhere, one road in. The guy who built it went bust and ended up in jail or something."

"I don't suppose I can GPS it?" she asked, holding up her phone for emphasis.

"Wouldn't know, but if you got a map I can show you where it is."

"Haven't got a map," she admitted.

Reaching past her, he plucked a road map from the wire spinner rack to her left.

"Two ninety-nine," he said, holding it up for emphasis. "Plus tax."

The additions Big Guy added to Nancy's map – with a magic marker – seemed to lead nowhere, until she reached the terminus of his thick red line and found the road she was looking for. Undesignated, unlit, camouflaged by darkness, she could have driven past it a dozen times and never known it was there. Turning in, she immediately came up against a perfunctory wooden barricade.

NO HIGHWAY EXIT – PRIVATE PROPERTY – NO TRESPASSING

She climbed out of the car to move it aside.

And that's when the stench hit her,

Rotten meat, intermingled with a musky, animal scent. She gagged.

Roadkill, she guessed. She held her breath as she moved the barricade. Her father had an old 45 record that he used to play when she was a kid, a novelty song about a dead skunk in the road. Smiling at the memory, she struggled to recall the lyrics.

Off road, in the darkness, there was a pinpoint of red.

What the hell?

She squinted, staring into the darkness across acres of tall, black grass, rustling in a light wind underneath an Oxford blue sky dense with unfamiliar stars. She felt like she was on another planet. An alien. An intruder.

There it was again. Two points of light, actually, red-orange, an indeterminate distance away in the field flanking the road.

Eyes. She could almost but not quite discern the dark bulk behind them.

An animal, the size of a largish dog, its eyes catching stray light from her high beams and throwing it back.

She sensed rather than heard a low, throaty rumble. A warning.

She backed up slowly, watching it. Just a feral stray. Likely the author of the dead animal she was smelling. Probably, it worried that she was going to make off with its dinner. It wouldn't approach her if she just...

It one smooth, fluid motion, the eyes rose up, into the air, to a height of six feet or more.

Like the dog(?) had suddenly stood up on its hind legs.

With a squeak, she dove into the driver's seat, slammed the door, and gunned it, her tires chirping briefly, as if her little car were far too proper to do anything so vulgar as actually "peel out". Her eyes darted to the rearview, where far too many episodes of *Supernatural* had her primed to see some *thing* loping after her, jaws slavering, eyes aflame.

There was nothing there, of course.

It was only a wild dog. A wild dog, an overactive imagination, and just maybe a teensy, tiny, subconscious urge to be rescued by Sam and Dean.

A minute passed. Two. Nancy had no way of knowing this of course, but her experience driving down the access road was very different from Abby's when the latter drove to and from "work" each day. Nancy saw no construction, no earth movers or other equipment, no framework skeleton of new neighborhoods springing up around the initial seven houses already completed. Whether this phantom construction was all a contrived illusion for the benefit of Abby and the others, or whether it was a dream – the optimistic dream, perhaps, of a sentient construct or an aggregate of constructs or something far stranger than that, something entirely beyond our comprehension – it was *not* objective reality. In reality, the road remained as it had always been: flanked by unkempt, overgrown fields, acres of wild scrub stretching as far as the eye could see, home to rat and snake and ground-nesting bird. Rarely disturbed by man. Numbing in its sameness.

Just ahead, something reared up on the left side of the road and Nancy slammed on her brakes.

It was a tractor. Pulled off to the side of the road. Just some farmer's tractor. Well-maintained, unremarkable. Likely the owner had had some sort of mechanical trouble and had to pull over and walk from here.

And yet.

And yet.

She was shaking, she realized. Her arms were covered in goose flesh.

Jesus Christ. That tractor. That *fucking*

tractor.

"*Oh God*," she moaned. She was crying. It was terrible. Unnatural. That tractor *didn't belong here*. It wasn't right and now *they* were going to take her, and she couldn't stop them.

Her car died, the engine first, then the lights. The last thing to wink out was the dash clock. It was 8:52.

Lights ahead, finally. Street lamps and... she'd found it! Even in the dark she recognized the site from the pictures she'd seen online. And were there lights on inside a couple of the houses? They actually had power out here? Or maybe the people Abby was with had hooked up generators or something. She checked the time on the dash.

2:58?

But...

Nancy slowed to a stop, pulled off the road near the entrance to the cul-de-sac. A plaque mounted on a low brick wall identified the neighborhood as "Inmoss Estates".

How could it be three o'clock in the morning? It wasn't quite nine when she'd located the access road. Could she have really spaced out for five hours? Impossible. She would have driven – she checked the tripometer – a lot further than four miles. The dash clock must be wonky. Didn't it flick out for a second just before...?

There was a tight feeling in her chest, an instant of terror that was gone even before she recognized it.

Well, no matter. She was here. And, holy shit, that was Abby's car, parked in the first drive on the left! Won't she be surprised? Climbing out of her car, Nancy found herself clutching the mixed nuts she'd bought, and the marked-up road map. Not much of a housewarming gift, but...

Housewarming?

What was she thinking? Abby didn't *live* here. Nobody lived here. They...

Porch lights winked on, lighting stoops. One at a time, circling the cul-de-sac. What in the world? Some sort of neighborhood-wide security system? Wait, they were out here hunting ghosts, right? Maybe she'd tripped a motion sensor or something. Maybe she was live on ghost-cam right now.

She certainly felt like she was being watched. No, more than that; like she was being watching by someone who had been stalking her online for some time and knew far too much about her. She fumbled out her phone, not sure if she was going to call 911 but feeling the need to be ready.

No service.

Of course.

She was in the yard now, staring at the front door. Abby's car crouched in the driveway to her right.

It's too late to knock, she thought. *I should probably just kill myself.*

Wait, what?

She started as the front door swung open, slowly, creaking loudly on corny horror movie hinges.

A light flicked on inside – a single bulb, bare, hanging from the ceiling – illuminating the entranceway and a dim hallway beyond. But no one was there.

"Abby?" she tried.

Silence.

She took a hesitant step forward. The bare bulb swung back and forth, back and forth, as if caught in a breeze. Air conditioner, maybe?

A strange thing popped, unbidden, into Nancy's mind. It was a fish. Specifically, a fish she'd once seen on the Discovery Channel. It had a luminescent growth sprouting from the top of its head, and it waggled this in front of its mouth to lure prey inside. Body almost spherical. Enormous, nearly vertical mouth. Dead, milky-white eyes. Long, thin, uncountable teeth, like organic needles. It was a deep-sea fish, mercifully tiny. She couldn't quite remember the name.

That's what the swaying light bulb reminded her of.

This time she took a step back. Except she didn't, she'd actually taken another step forward.

The swinging light bulb was hypnotizing. She felt drawn to it, like a moth.

She closed her eyes, willed herself to stop walking.

For a moment, she could still see a ghostly afterimage of the light, swinging behind her eyelids. Then nothing. Darkness. Silence. The air was sticky and heavy and carried a faint scent of fish, presumably all the way from the coast.

She stood there, eyes closed, for several seconds.

"Okay," she finally said aloud. "Fuck this."

Eyes still closed, she turned around, a full 180 degrees.

She opened her eyes. The house, the open door, the beckoning light all safely behind her now.

In front of her, something not so dissimilar to that fish she'd seen on the Discovery Channel. Not dissimilar, but, somehow, infinitely worse. And considerably larger.

She didn't scream, merely gurgled. An instant later she was enveloped in moist, soggy darkness, inundated with the stench of rot and decay and the sea, hundreds of bony needles piercing her back and stomach, severing her, her legs kicking in the open air and then *separating*... oh god she was in two pieces, the uppermost tumbling down some unimaginable *thing's* gullet, the bottom half quietly oozing her innards all over the front lawn...

Her eyes snapped open.

Daylight. She'd fallen asleep in the front seat of the car. She reached down, squeezed her thighs to make sure her legs were still there, lifted her shirt looking for teeth marks.

Jesus *fucking* **Christ**.

She'd never had a nightmare that real. Sitting up, she blinked in the bright sunlight, gave herself a moment to remember where the hell she was.

She was parked in front of her own house.

She checked her phone, compared the time to the dash clock. Double-checked the date.

It was almost noon, exactly twenty-four hours after she'd climbed into her car to go looking for Abby.

Nope.

Nope nope nope nope.

She went inside, showered, pulled her hair back into a ponytail because that was quickest, light makeup, yoga pants and uggs because he liked the way she looked in yoga pants and uggs, and drove straight to Devon's. He was a writer, so he was always home during the day. Her place was being, uh, fumigated, so could she stay there for a few days? Sure, of course. They popped popcorn and watched Netflix and snuggled, and that night they made love and it was nice and she stayed longer than a few days and eventually he just asked her to move in.

So things worked out pretty okay for Nancy.

Still, it would be a long time before she was comfortable being alone at night.

PART TWO

THEN/NOW

———— 1

If Ahmad and his team really meant to be scientific about this, they weren't doing a very good job. For starters, their undergrad assistants, all three of them, were clearly hungover from the night before. And they weren't the only ones. More to the point, however: No one seemed to agree on what, exactly, they should do next. Everyone had his or her or their own pet methodology, and watching them put these into play was like watching ants who'd suddenly become enlightened and valued individuality over the communal nest scamper about, pursuing opposing agendas and getting in each other's way. Itsuki Kobayashi's activities, at least, had the sheen of scientific methodology, as he went from house to house, setting up remote recording devices – video, audio, atmospheric, and more – that could be monitored from the Nerve Center. The others, though...

Jasper and that weird gothy chick Winter were

just wandering around, getting "impressions". The only "impression" Abby got was that they were making most of it up. The Remington siblings and Lionel both relied on tech, sporting similar gizmos as she'd seen on any given ghost chasers TV show, the only difference being that Lionel's were all installed on his phone. They measured EMF readings and noted "cold spots" and the twins spent an inordinate amount of time taking pictures – hundreds of them – of that light bulb that had flickered on yesterday. In fact, the twins pretty much staked out the house where the light bulb incident occurred, claiming it as their own. They even ran Suki out before he could install his monitoring devices.

Even Professor Mahmoud, their ostensible leader, went his own way, breaking out something he referred to as a "spirit box" and striding over to the house directly across from the Nerve Center, with a clearly miserable Hannah in tow.

"What is a 'spirit box'?" Abby asked Shane as she watched them cross the street. The Indian shook his head.

"It's the stupidest goddamned..." He took a deep breath. "Okay, a 'spirit box' is just a receiver that scans radio waves and plays a snippet of each one before moving on to the next. It's basically a radio, but it only picks up each station for an instant. The idea is that spirits can talk to you via the white noise this produces, but you're picking up *terrestrial radio* so *of course* your brain will pick out the occasional word, even if it's just a fortuitous collusion. It's akin to rapidly flipping through TV stations, recognizing Betty White and Bea Arthur as they flash by, and citing this as evidence that your house is haunted by the Golden Girls. It is, literally, the dumbest thing the ghost hunting set have come up with yet. And that's saying something."

"So worth watching?" Abby grinned.

"Oh, absolutely."

She hurried to catch up with Ahmad and the hungover redhead, but when she tried the front door of the house they'd disappeared into, it was locked. She raised a hand to knock, then hesitated.

It might be a lot more interesting to see how this plays out when he doesn't know he's got an audience. She hopped off the stoop and cautiously circled the house instead. A quick glance through the front window, into the living room, revealed nothing. Window sure was clean, though, she realized. Like someone had just Windexed it. She wondered, absently, if the undergrad assistants hadn't been tasked with this. *They came to bust ghosts. They ended up doing windows.* Continuing around the right side of the house she passed the chimney, then reached a second window. She could hear voices inside. One of them was definitely Ahmad.

"...rare opportunity and you quibble over trifles," he was saying. Abby, crouching down, carefully peeped in over the sill. Hannah and the professor were in what appeared to be the dining room. The spirit box – it looked like a small transistor radio – sat on a long, functional table that dominated the room. *Hannah and the Professor* would be a good name for a sitcom, Abby reflected.

"I'm hungover," Hannah protested, brushing a stray length of red hair out of her face.

"Well it's not like you have to *do* anything. Just stand there," Ahmad said. Reaching past her, he flicked the spirit box on. It began producing white noise immediately, static, mostly, like a radio not tuned to any particular station. If you really listened – and had a good imagination – the occasional word was discernible. Abby thought she heard "Budweiser", for instance.

Then Abby gasped.

Because Ahmad wasn't paying any attention to the spirit box at all.

He was too busy taking Hannah's shirt off.

The redhead didn't resist, but she didn't look too happy about it, either. Her bra was next, and then Ahmad just stood there, staring off into space, listening to the spirit box while he absently fondled his assistant's breasts.

Jesus H. Perv, Abby thought, ducking out of sight. *What a disgusting shit*. She couldn't bear to watch any more of this vile display, but she listened for a while, as the spirit box hissed and fuzzed and occasionally sputtered something almost but not quite intelligible. She thought she picked out the phrase "Chow chow chow" once, but even that took some mental gymnastics. Christ, did Mahmoud even buy into his own bullshit, or was this all just an excuse to get into his credulous assistants' pants? She wondered, briefly, if she should possibly gather some photographic evidence of his reprehensible behavior, but Hannah was over eighteen and likely all Abby would accomplish would be humiliating the poor girl. She decided against it. Instead, she moved on, creeping around the back of the house so that she could come around the other side, away from any prying eyes that might be looking after *her* prying eyes. She duck-walked beneath the second dining room window, the one facing the rear of the house, and then scampered to the far side of the building before she came back around front.

Just in time to see Rachel step out of the RV. Half tee and cut-off jeans, braless, off-brand western-look ankle boots. A white trash dream, even with the unfortunate facial scarring. Composing herself and quickly putting some distance between her person and what she now thought of as "Mahmoud's Pleasure Palace", Abby raised one hand and called out to her. Rachel's eyes narrowed at her approach.

"What do you want, Little Miss..." She grasped for a press-oriented reference, but anything appropriate eluded her. Instead, she simply let the question trail off into a sneer.

"I want what any reporter wants," Abby said

through an artificial smile. "Your story."

"I told you my story."

"But it's not over yet, right?"

"It is for you," Rachel said. She paused dramatically. "Unless you want to watch."

"Er..." Abby managed. This had caught her off guard. Now Rachel smiled.

"That's it, isn't it? You want to *watch*."

"No, I..."

Suddenly Rachel was right up in her face, pressed against her body. Abby could feel Rachel's pert nipples through her shirt, taste the chemical mint of fresh toothpaste on her breath. Her hair smelled like hand soap. Slowly, Rachel wrapped one bare leg around Abby's own.

Please kiss me, Abby thought.

"Stop playing games," she actually said.

"But that's what this is, isn't it?" Rachel said, backing off. The sweep of her arm took in the whole of the neighborhood. "Just one big game?"

"Not to me it isn't." Abby wasn't even sure what she meant by that, but she felt like she had to say *something* defiant. Rachel was unnerving the shit out of her.

The two women stared at each other for a moment.

"I like you," Rachel decided, then turned and sashayed away.

$$\underline{\qquad\qquad} \mathbf{2}$$

Saturday night in the cul.

--

Abilene Beaumont tossed and turned in her sleep, her subconscious wholly rejecting everything her senses had processed during waking hours. In her dreams, she sat in an unfamiliar bedroom, an incessant rapping on the door. The bedside phone rang and she picked it up, only to hear her own voice repeating, over and over, "Don't answer the door! Do *not* answer that door!"

--

Patches the dog worried at the mysterious cupboard his owner refused to open, while said owner struggled to turn his cabinet-style monstrosity of a television around so that it faced the wall.

--

Itsuki Kobayashi slept soundly, wholly

unaware that his wife – who was, in fact, not his wife, though only she recognized this – had, once again, slipped out of the house to meet the crazy woman who lived in the RV parked behind the development.

--

Lionel Holland stared in fascinated terror as a phalanx of shadows – shadows with no recognizable source – reenacted the horrors of history on his bedroom wall.

--

College students Emily and Madison were hosting another Saturday night rager. Emily drank shots with a gaggle of Sigma girls until she hurled, and Madison eventually went upstairs with a strange boy, leaving the party to careen to a conclusion without her. Yet anyone peeping in on these festivities would have been baffled, because the two girls were clearly alone in the house, blaring music, binge drinking, and interacting with invisible people who weren't there.

--

Hannah got home late, having spent the evening researching undetectable poisons on one of the public computers at school, so that the search history couldn't be traced back to her. Professor Ahmad Mahmoud, the inspiration for this, was already asleep.

--

Robert and Roberta Remington made love, and then, as usual, Roberta threw up.

—— *3*

Everyone had scattered, leaving Abby standing there, alone, in the middle of the street. The last to go were the twins, who leapt into their car and left the development entirely. "Where are *you* off to?" Abby had asked through the open window as they crept past.

"Denny's!" Rob answered.

"And a shower!" Bobbi shouted across him from the passenger seat. Then they were gone.

Should've asked them to bring me back a decent coffee, Abby thought. There was lousy coffee up for grabs over at the Nerve Center, but Abby decided against it and strolled down the center of the cul instead, circumventing the first, smaller center island she came to but then stopping at the edge of one of the two larger ones. The "eyes". She ran a finger down the trunk of one of the dead trees jutting forth from it. Pity. But they weren't all dead, she realized. In fact, the trees in the interior seemed to be doing rather well; it was just the outer ring that was dead. How had she not noticed this before? Slipping between two of the dead specimens, she carefully stepped into the middle of the island.

It was kind of beautiful. The trees were resplendent with green, fresh green, and thick, fairy tale vines that seemed to envelop everything. She wouldn't have been surprised to find Sleeping Beauty stashed in here, pristine, delicate, forever inviolate in her glass coffin. She took a long moment to appreciate that strangely reinvigorating scent of growing things, the dappled sunlight leaking from above, then turned to leave.

And couldn't find her way out.

Three steps, four, a dozen. The little island of foliage wasn't more than twenty feet in diameter but she couldn't see the street, the houses, anywhere, in any direction.

Her chest tightened with panic.

And unfounded or not, it was true panic. Because she sensed a *vastness* around her, as one might feel in the depths of the wilderness, far from mankind's negligible cities and his adorable conviction that he's somehow conquered nature. She suddenly recognized the fragility of it all; the wild places almost pressing in on their laughable "civilization" on all sides; the *things* that dwelt there just waiting for...

She closed her eyes, choked back a scream.

Okay, this was insane. You don't get lost in a

tiny copse of trees growing out of a traffic island in the middle of an unfinished housing development.

You just *don't*.

She opened her eyes and she was right, she hadn't.

She was two long strides from the concrete, the road proper. Always had been. Nevertheless she quickly extricated herself, before she wasn't anymore.

Jesus God in Heaven.

Was this location *really* haunted? Is that what that was? It felt... bigger than that, somehow; as if ghosts, demons, UFOs and Loch Ness Monsters and all the rest of it weren't enough to define what was happening here, what was happening at all the heres like this place where people experienced something wholly outside the normal. There was a strange sense that she was on the verge of an intellectual breakthrough, an epoch-defining epiphany dancing infuriatingly at the edge of her consciousness like a name that you can't quite recall even though it's on the tip of your tongue.

Then it was gone.

I just got lost on a traffic island, she thought.

A funny story to tell later.

This was all she ultimately took from the experience. All they allowed her to take.

$$\underline{\qquad\qquad} 4$$

When, well after dawn, Winter slipped back into the neighborhood proper, she found her immediate neighbor sitting on the curb in front of his house, clutching a mug of something that someone considerably more generous might consider coffee, and staring off into space like a shell-shocked war vet. At first she couldn't even recall his name, but then it came to her. Lionel.

"I think my house is haunted," he said, locking eyes with her as she tried to pass with a noncommittal nod. Like maybe she could do something about it. Like maybe he remembered that she *could*, theoretically, do something about it. She froze. Was this a trick? Maybe. But at this point... It had all gone too far. It needed to end, if it could be ended, soon. And for this, they needed allies.

"Follow me," she said, without breaking her stride. Instead of going into "her" house she walked past it, through the back yard (they had a swing set back there – or a simulacrum of one, anyway – she realized; why would they need a swing set?) and into the land surrounding the cul. Construction, in various stages, as far as the eye could see. Duplicate neighborhoods going up along both sides of the road. Earth movers and workers and shouts, the whine of tools and the smell of sawdust. She glanced back to see if Lionel was following. He was. When she got a fair distance from their own street she stopped and waited for him to catch up. He'd abandoned his coffee, she noticed.

Now, which one was he? What was his defining...?

Oh, yes. Apps. All of his ghost hunting tools were apps.

"Do you have your phone?" Winter asked.

"My...?" The question seemed to confuse him, but then he checked his pockets.

"No."

"Do you know where it is?"

Again the confusion.

"I..."

"Never mind. It's gone, I'm sure. Too much of a prompt."

One of the distant workmen took note of them, gave Winter the once-over, and wolf-whistled.

"Your house is haunted," she said. "It's haunted as fuck."

"Then you've seen things too?"

"Try to remember, Lionel. Can you do that for

me?"

He stared at her blankly. She sighed.

"You have to get past all this," she said, indicating the construction in particular. "It's an illusion. Part of the little scenario they've fabricated for us."

"I don't understand," Lionel said.

Without another word, Winter unfastened her belt and let the loose-fitting jeans she wore drop to the ground. Stepping out of them, she removed her shirt and tossed that aside as well. She wore no bra.

Another whistle from one of the laborers, more aggressive this time, followed by a couple of cheers. The words *it off* floated back to them on the wind.

"Watch," Winter said. Clad only in her panties, she turned and strode aggressively towards the slack-jawed, cat-calling construction workers. Three of them. Two dropped the shovels they were holding and moved to meet her. Too slim, too pale, eyes and ears a tad too large, she was far from the current, limited, cultural ideal. But at that moment: lithe; near-naked; bare feet dark with fresh, clean earth; white hair stained orange-pink by the rising sun, she transcended that.

She was a goddess.

And when the first of the men reached out and touched her, with his vulgar, mortal hands, he was consumed.

And with him went the illusion; the

construction, the laborers, their tools and machines – all gone.

Winter turned, walked back to Lionel.

"You see?" she said. "It's showing us what it *wants*. What it hopes to achieve."

"I... remember..." he said. "You, you're the psychic. The other psychic. There were two of you..."

Winter nodded.

"Jasper," she reminded him. "He's dead."

"No, I've seen him, walking his dog. Today. Not even twenty minutes ago."

Winter shook her head.

"They got him first, early on. They knew he'd be able to see through the illusion. They don't know that I can too."

"They?"

"They. It. Whatever's in control of this place." She bent down to pick up her top. Lionel closed the distance in a flash and before she could process the fact that he was assaulting her the blade was already in her belly. With a single, smooth motion he drew it from her navel to her sternum, opening her up. She fell against him, eyes wide, soaking him in wet and warmth, hands grasping at his clothing as she slid down his body.

"Urk," she said as she crumpled to the ground. She could see things trailing out into the grass; glistening things that should have been inside her.

Oh Gaia no.

"Sorry, not sorry," Lionel said robotically.

He wiped the bloody blade off on his slacks, then tossed it aside. He stared at Winter's body for several minutes, not quite processing what he was seeing, then turned and walked back to the cul.

— **5**

Abby let her feet carry her where they would, and a couple of minutes later she found herself in the house at the head of the cul. Hearing footsteps above her, she walked up one flight of stairs, then two, and ended up in the attic, where she discovered Suki, carefully adjusting a mounted camera. He was singing softly to himself. That old Toto song "Pamela", except he was substituting the word *Canada* for *Pamela*. "Howdy," he smiled when Abby appeared. "How's your morning going?"

Well, I just watched our fearless leader molest a teenager, a girl acted like she was going to mouth-rape me and I think I might've liked it, and I got lost in a twenty-square-foot patch of foliage, she thought.

"Fine," she said.

"Glad to hear it." Aside from a half-empty bottle of Vitamin Water sitting on the floor, the attic was bare. But bright morning sunlight streamed through the quarter moon windows, making the wood all but glow, and the effect was rather cheery. "Could you stand in the middle of the room?" Suki asked her.

"Sure."

He nudged the camera so that it was pointing right at her. Now she could see the tiny red power light, dutifully blinking. "Wave," he smiled. "You're on *Candid Camera*." He frowned, fiddled with the mount again. "Hopefully," he added.

"Are you going to set up surveillance in all the houses?" Abby asked.

"Already done," Suki said. "Except the Standoff House, as they've been calling it. The Remingtons have pretty much claimed that one for their own." He was clearly irritated by this. "Not very scientific," he opined. Satisfied with the camera placement, he sat down, Indian style, and took a long pull from his Vitamin Water. Cool blueberry-lavender flavor, whatever that meant.

"Up for a quick interview?" Abby pulled out her phone.

"Sure."

"So," she tapped the Record Sound icon as she sat down next to him. "What do *you* think is happening here? Do you really think this entire development is haunted?"

"In a way. I think it was, quite frankly, inevitable."

"How so?"

"Are you familiar with the concept of the doppelganger, the double?"

"Sort of. Like your twin, right? They say everyone has a look-alike somewhere in the world."

"Not exactly. The true doppelganger is more of a projection, like a ghost, but the ghost of someone who is still alive. Maybe an astral projection, or maybe, as some folklore suggests, a harbinger – your ghost is out roaming around because you're not long for this world."

"My grandmother always said that if you met your double, you were going to die soon."

"Yes. Now let's extrapolate from that. Have you ever heard the word *tulpa*?"

Abby shook her head, then remembered she was recording. "No," she said out loud.

"Well the tulpa is a similar sort of projection. A ghost, but one we create ourselves, simply by believing that it exists. Let me tell you a story. Back in the days of the Cold War, it wasn't unusual for the Soviet Union to draw up maps containing various forms of misdirection. Features indicated where no such feature existed, entire areas scrambled or misnamed or left off the map entirely. Petty obfuscations, to keep the West from learning too much. Well, there were towns on some of these maps that were entirely imaginary, and yet in 1996 a group of paranormal investigators from Great Britain visited one of these towns, a non-existent village identified on a topographical survey as Sterga-Kironovo. They took readings, took pictures, walked the eerily deserted streets, watched in awe as the whole of it flickered in and out of existence around them. It was real, or almost real, solely because it was on that map. Because enough people *believed* it was real. The entire town was a tulpa."

Tulpa City, Oklahoma, Abby thought to herself.

"So that's your theory of ghosts?" she asked.

"Indeed. If there are any ghosts here, we brought them with us."

—— *6*

"I think even vehement believers are convinced, deep down inside, that ghosts don't really exist," Lionel said. He'd returned home, showered, burned the clothes he'd been wearing in the fireplace. There was no immediate evidence that not forty minutes ago he'd gutted an attractive young woman like a pig and left her for dead.

"Oh?"

"Yeah. *That's* why they scare us, the real reason. Because when one shows up, it's like reality is broken. Our brains can't handle that."

"I see."

"It's true. I mean, no one's ever been *hurt* by a ghost, not really. Maybe they get hurt running away, but that's it."

"Are you sure?"

"Pretty sure." Lionel sat down on the bed, pulled on a fresh pair of jeans. "I mean, you hear about things, forces grabbing people or pushing them down the stairs, but likely it's just hysteria, unreliable testimony. Fake news. I figure, either ghosts can touch us, or they can't. If they can't, we've got nothing to worry about, right? And if they can, well, then we should be able to touch them, too, so what's stopping us from just beating the bejeebus out of one?" He was speaking with a machine gun rapidity now, as if his thoughts were outracing his ability to express them. "What I'm saying is that, worst case scenario, we can still defend ourselves! It's harder to be afraid of something when you know that you can defend yourself."

"But you are afraid, aren't you?"

"Why should I be?" Still rapid-fire. "I've never done anything wrong in my life! In second grade, when everyone made fun of Pete Orlowski, made him cry, I went up to him and told him I'd be his friend. The other boys ostracized me, but I didn't care. Because it was the *right* thing to do."

"You're babbling."

"Am I?"

"Maybe you were seen. Followed."

Followed.

"The Lengua," Lionel said, swallowing hard.

"What's that?"

"When Lengua huntsmen killed a rhea, they would use its feathers to create little decoys so that the bird's spirit wouldn't follow them back to the village. Oh God. Oh Christ. What am I going to do?"

No answer. Which shouldn't have been surprising, because he was alone in the house.

_______ 7

"Hello."

Jasper, deep in his shtick, started, but Winter only turned and smiled.

"Hello, Ms. DeVries."

"Rachel, please." She climbed the last few stairs and joined them in the attic.

"We didn't hear you come in," Jasper said, a bit irritably.

"Oh, you didn't know I was coming?" An obvious dig. Jasper didn't take the bait.

"Jasper's reading the room," Winter explained. "We decided to start up here and work our way down, one room at a time."

"Let me guess," Rachel said. "He senses _two_ spirits, one good, one **eeevil**. The good one is a child."

"Why don't you go fuck yourself?" Jasper said mildly.

"Actually," Rachel said, locking eyes with

Winter. "That's why I'm here. A word?"

"Sure."

The two women drifted downstairs.

"I won't mince," Rachel said. "Are you for reals, or are you just a sexier take on John Edward?"

"If you hadn't thrown *sexy* in there I'd be unbelievably offended."

"Good. There's no telling what these clowns are already stirring up around here, so I'm going to do my thing tonight. I'd like you to tag along, if you're willing."

"Tag along physically, or in your noggin?"

"Both."

Winter considered for a moment.

"What, exactly, is your *thing*, anyway?" she finally asked. "I mean, are you even a sensitive, or...?"

"You know what happened to me?"

"I know what you say happened to you."

"Well it's going to happen again, only this time **I'm** going to be in control."

"Why?"

"Why, what?"

"Why would you want to..." Winter hesitated, choosing her words "...copulate with an entity?"

"Have you ever tried it? It's divine."

"I thought you were raped."

"I can't defend that aspect of it. I won't say it wasn't a violation, the worst kind of violation. But the underlying..." She paused, her eyes glittering with a near madness. "If I'd been

116

willing, it would have been *so good*. Can you understand that? It felt like... being chosen. Like the Virgin Mary must have felt, you know? Scared to death but just so damn *honored*..."

Wasn't there some psychological thing where the victim of a violent crime sometimes blames herself? That must be what's happening here, Winter decided.

Aloud, she said, "Sure." Because she felt like she had to say *something*.

"The point is, I'm going to do it. And I'd like you to be there. In my head."

"When?"

"Late, after everyone else turns in. I'm inviting the journalist, too. We'll conduct a little ceremony to draw it in, then you two can both do *your* thing. She gets her story, you experience the most intense, unique paranormal-psychic encounter imaginable."

"And you get 'lucky'."

"Jealous? Maybe he'll bring a friend."

"No thanks."

"So you'll do it?"

"I think you're crazy. I think you have an unhealthy obsession, brought on by trauma, that's driving you to toy with something you can't possibly hope to control. I think a *best* case scenario is that this entire investigation is compromised and only a couple of people get hurt."

"That sounds like a yes."

"It is."

——— *8*

In the end she opted for antifreeze, mostly because it was so accessible, but also because the articles she found online suggested that it was difficult for forensics to detect. She split what she determined to be a fatal dose between three cups of coffee. Ahmad barely noticed, just once mentioning that it tasted too sweet.

If she expected him to collapse immediately, hands grasping his throat, she was disappointed. He pecked her on the cheek and left for work.

But that night he was home an hour early, citing an upset stomach, reeling slightly as if drunk. He curled up on the couch, soaked in sweat, asked Hannah to bring him some water. She brought him a Pepsi instead, laced with more antifreeze.

Five hours later he had a seizure and soiled himself. He began ranting, wildly, about "them", finally clarifying that "them" were dozens of spirits, surrounding him, closing in. He seized again, vomited all over the living room carpet, fell off the couch into his own sick, tried to crawl to the bathroom while continuing to wail about being surrounded by the dead.

It wasn't neat. It was horrible and messy and ugly and it took him another twenty hours to die. Hannah spent most of this time curled up in a ball, locked in the upstairs bedroom, wishing she'd clobbered him with a baseball bat instead. Trying to distance herself from the deed had only made it so much worse.

Finally it was over, and she realized that killing a person is the easy part. It's disposing of the body that's difficult.

She hadn't anticipated the necessity of this. She'd poisoned him, so she thought she would simply report his "mysterious" death to the authorities and the worst of it would be over. She hadn't expected him to take over a day to succumb, to puke and piss and shit everywhere in the process, to flail around in hallucinatory terror, thoroughly trashing a significant portion of the house. She couldn't possibly sell the lie that she didn't know there was something wrong. Better she had stabbed him and then claimed he'd been beating her. Now, she was fucked.

But maybe not. Certainly she wasn't going to give up. She'd come this far.

In the wee hours of the morning, she hauled Ahmad out through the kitchen door, into the back yard. It was slow going. He was heavy, dead weight, and the smell and the reality of what she'd done conspired to gag her. More than once, she had to walk away, gulp in deep breaths of fresh, night air. Two hours later she'd managed to drag the body deep into the fields behind the development.

And that's where Rachel found her.

$$—— 9$$

She looks pretty good in those cut-off shorts. If she wasn't your sister...

What the fuck?

Rob stepped away from the videocam's viewfinder. He even turned his head, pointedly not looking as Bobbi bent over to get a still shot of the broken window with her Nikon Z6. Against the wall, the rest of their gear, including cots and sleeping bags. Not only had they claimed exclusivity regarding the Standoff House, they'd essentially moved in.

Where did *that* fucked-up thought come from, Rob wondered. And why had he addressed himself in the third person?

"Are you videoing?" Bobbi asked, her back still to him.

"Not yet," he managed. She really did have nice legs, he conceded. Great smile. She was going to make some guy very happy someday.

Kind of unfair, isn't it?

What?

You've known her her whole life.

Of course. I'm her *brother.*

Dibs.

What?

*You should have **dibs**.* The last word drawn out, like a hiss.

Holy shit.

"Something's trying to communicate with me," he said breathlessly. Bobbi spun around.

"What?" she gasped excitedly.

Gasped. Excited.

"Yes, right now. It's putting, er, icky thoughts into my head."

"Are you sure those aren't your own icky thoughts?" Bobbi grinned.

"I'm serious. This is..." he hesitated, opted to keep it vague "...vile stuff. We need one of the sensitives."

"Want me to shimmy out of these shorts so you can have a little feast?"

Oh my god.

"W-What?"

"I said, do you want me to run get one?"

He was sweating, his pulse rate had skyrocketed.

"Yeah, hurry."

"Are you okay?"

"I'm okay!" he snapped. "Hurry!"

"Alright, geez." She trotted out the door.

To his great shame, he zoomed the video

camera in on her ass and followed her as she jogged up the street. He didn't even realize what his other hand was doing until he'd climaxed.

10

"My great-auntie was from the old country – that's what my family called Rhode Island – and she insisted that a spot of tea solves anything." Rachel set the not-quite-steaming cup in front of Hannah. She'd heated it up on a cordless hot plate. The RV's house battery was long since depleted.

"Thanks," Hannah managed. She noticed that the scarred-up woman hadn't fixed a cup for herself.

"Oh, I never touch the stuff," Rachel said, reading her mind. Or the look on her face, anyway.

They sat in silence for a time.

"You're... Daphne, right? I mean, that's what they called you."

"Hannah," the redhead clarified.

"Right. So, wanna tell me why you offed the Professor, Ginger?"

Hannah looked sick. Too soon to be flippant, apparently. Rachel changed tactics.

"If it'll put your mind at ease, it's not your fault. Really. He was probably possessed. Or you were. Is any of it coming back to you at all?"

"Yes," Hannah said. It was, in bits and pieces. She was Professor Mahmoud's assistant, not his live-in lover. They'd come here to hunt ghosts.

Rachel waited.

"How did this happen?" Hannah finally asked. "What's going on?"

"We opened a door, I guess. Or maybe we just made it too easy for them."

"Them?"

"You know – the spirits; the demons; the indefinable, otherworldly whatsits. Whatever."

"But why..."

"After the shitstorm, everyone who wasn't dead just wandered into one of the houses and set up shop like they'd been living there for the duration. Those things got in your heads, somehow; convinced the lot of you that you were just a bunch of typical, neurotic suburbanites. All but Winter. She duped them with those River Tam powers of hers."

Hannah didn't know what a River Tam was, but let it go.

"Winter's the emo girl, right?" she asked instead. "With the silver hair." Rachel nodded.

"But why?" Hannah repeated. "Why do all this, make us into people we're not?"

"To torture you. To make you as miserable as

125

possible and then feed off that misery. That's what Winter says, anyway."

"And you and Winter weren't affected because you're psychic."

Rachel looked away.

"*Winter* wasn't affected because she's psychic. They've already taken everything they could possibly take from me."

Silence, endless and uncomfortable. Then Hannah remembered.

"What about the other psychic? The one with the little dog that kept shitting all over the RV?" She remembered this well – she'd had to clean up after the miserable bugger. Wracking her brain, it finally came to her. "Jasper."

"He's dead," Rachel said.

"No, he isn't! I see him all the time, walking that stupid dog."

"Are you sure? Winter told me he was dead."

"He's not, I swear."

"Listen to me," Rachel said, taking her hand. "I know your first instinct is to turn your back on this place and just keep walking, but I need your help. Those other two assistants, they're classmates of yours, right? Maybe friends? *They* need your help."

Hannah started crying. Or maybe she'd been crying this whole time. Rachel was the first to admit that she didn't score top marks in empathy.

"I just want to go home!" the redhead wept. "I want my Dad!"

"We're past the point where *Dad* can help," Rachel said.

"He'll know what to do..." Hannah insisted.

"Does he know if quicklime will dissolve a body? Because that's something he'll need to know. It doesn't, by the way. That's a freebie for you."

Rachel just was being mean at this point, but to her surprise this actually brought the crying girl up short. She had her attention, so she quickly exploited the situation.

"I'll help you, okay? We'll burn the body, scatter the bones. Animals will eat the rest. I'll show you what to do. You'll be okay. But I need something in return. Nothing bad. I just want you to get Jasper, tonight, and bring him here. Feed him any bullshit you have to to get him to come. Will you do that for me?"

"Why can't you do it?" Hannah asked, suspicious in spite of everything. No dummy, this one.

"I'm pretty sure **they** think I'm dead. If I blithely stroll back into their sphere of influence, that scuttles any advantage we might have."

Hannah didn't respond, but she was clearly weighing her options.

"It's a pretty good deal," Rachel prodded. "Harmless errand in exchange for a felony."

Hannah nodded. "Okay," she whispered. Then, louder, "Okay."

Rachel smiled. It had been so long it actually made the sides of her face hurt. Maybe, just maybe, with Winter *and* Jasper behind her, she could have her revenge. And if this pretty little redhead got smeared in the process, well, you had to break a few eggs, right?

11

Come nightfall, at Professor Mahmoud's suggestion, the lot of them gathered at the Nerve Center, crowding into a living room already compromised by supplies and monitoring equipment. The idea was to compare notes, but, for the most part, everyone just talked over one another. Suki had picked up some weird flashes in one of the houses that turned out to be an equipment issue. Jasper had "felt a presence". Rob Remington rather nervously admitted to some sort of semi-direct contact with *something*, but dodged any requests to elaborate. Shane made snide comments under his breath. It was all embarrassingly slapdash and unscientific, and Abby was kind of relieved when Winter, with a light jerk of her head, indicated that they step outside together.

Rachel was waiting for them.

"Hello, lover," she said to Abby.

"That's pretty presumptuous," Abby frowned.

"Is it?"

"Rachel has a proposition," Winter quickly interrupted. "She's going to attempt a summoning tonight. She, we, would like you there to record the event."

"It's what you wanted, isn't it?" Rachel cooed. "A Rachel DeVries exclusive?" She stepped forward, touched Abby's chest with her index finger.

"Why don't you drop the sex kitten act?"

"Why? Does it make you uncomfortable?"

It did, but Abby would never admit that.

"It's juvenile," she said instead.

And Rachel dropped it, just like that. Suddenly she was all business. Abby was surprised to find herself a little disappointed.

"Okay," Rachel said. "This is just the three of us. The house at the very head of the street, 3 AM. Bring your camera or your phone or whatever you use. And a tripod. Don't be late."

"What, exactly, am I going to be documenting?"

"Wear something sexy," Rachel replied, and strode off.

Both women watched her go, until she was out of sight behind the RV. They heard the door open and close. Jasper's dog, who had been locked inside the RV all day, greeted her excitedly.

"God damn is she weird," Abby said.

Weird, and dangerous, thought Winter.

———— *12*

It was dawn by the time Hannah left the RV, the sun hesitantly creeping over the horizon as if embarrassed. Hannah marched back through the field, soaking her shoes with dew, skirted "her" house, and paused on the sidewalk, examining the neighborhood in a new/old light. She felt like she'd woken up from a long, intense, and yet somehow mundane dream. It was still too early for anyone to be about, so she saw no one as she followed the walk the long way around, eyes repeatedly darting left, wary of the clumps of trees sprouting out of the larger pair of traffic islands. As if something would suddenly burst out of them, coming for her.

She stopped in front of Jasper's house.

"Okay," she said aloud.

Strolling up the walk, she knocked on the door.

His obnoxious little dog instantly kicked up a

ruckus, barking and ricocheting about.

She waited.

Nothing else.

Maybe he wasn't home.

This early, though? That seemed unlikely.

She tried the knob. Unlocked.

Slowly, she opened it.

The little dog scampered outside immediately, whining and bouncing up and down, excited to see her. Ignoring it, she stepped inside, leaving the door open.

The house was darkish, shades pulled, air musty and tinged with just a hint of something off-sweet and unpleasant. The dog whined again. "Shush," she told it. Creeping past the stairs, she stole a glance into the living room. Nothing unusual, except that the television – an old cabinet-style job – was turned so that it faced the wall. The dog scampered ahead, stopped, looked back. Like it wanted her to follow it.

So she did. Through the living room, the dining room, and into the kitchen.

The odd smell was stronger here.

The dog paused in front of the large floor-level cabinet, whined, looked at her expectantly. Maybe that's where Jasper kept its food, and it wanted breakfast.

Don't do it! her mind screamed, even as she was reaching for the latch.

Jasper's body was stuffed inside the cabinet. Weeks dead, mutilated almost beyond recognition.

She retched. The dog let out a long, mournful howl.

And in the living room something moved, thumped twice against the wall, then fell over with a heavy thud. There was a rush of air all around her as something spilled into the kitchen, dark shapes, not quite discernible, swirling and cavorting all around her, heavy with glee and anticipation. Jasper screamed. Not his body – it was well past the point of doing anything – but him nonetheless, somehow, as if he were standing next to her, invisible, and not dead and stuffed inside a cabinet. His dog pissed itself in terror and rocketed out of the room, through the dining room and out of sight, so quickly that Hannah would swear its feet never even touched the floor. There was motion all around her, as of a struggle she couldn't quite see or feel. "Please, no..." someone, not her, pleaded piteously.

Next door, standing on her porch smoking a morning cigarette, Abby watched with mild awe as Patches hurtled through Jasper's open front door, fully airborne, hit the ground running, took the corner at the end of the street like a motocross champ, and tore off down the access road at full speed. She barely had time to process this before she heard Hannah scream.

13

Individual investigations continued into the night, but everyone finally gave up the ghost, so to speak, around two. By the half hour, most were asleep, whether in the RV, camped out in one of the houses, or in the backseat of a car.

Most.

Abby set the LED lantern on the back of the toilet, flooding the bathroom with harsh, white light. Not the optimal lighting to apply makeup, but it would have to do. Why she felt the urge to make herself up for this, she didn't know. Or wouldn't admit to herself. She felt a flush of excitement as she dressed – an oversized t-shirt (men's, XXL) and the shortest shorts she had. She cringed at the stubble on her legs. Was there time to shave? Would Rachel...

She brought her own train of thought up short.

She wasn't doing this because she expected to see a ghost.

She was doing this because she had a crush on Rachel DeVries.

But that was okay.

Wasn't it?

Yes, yes it was, she decided as she scrutinized herself in the mirror above the sink.

Damn it, she really wanted to shave her legs. She had her Aveeno and a razor in her little emergency overnight bag, but there was no water. Maybe she could pop back into the Nerve Center and snag a bottle? Her hand automatically reached for the faucet and absently turned it on and off even as she considered this.

A nugget of liquid coughed out, startling her.

What the hell? She cautiously turned the handle again.

Clear, cool water poured out in a steady flow. But that was impossible, wasn't it?

She decided not to question her good fortune.

She shaved her legs.

14

Daphne? – no, Hannah – was in Jasper's house, and she looked like she'd seen a ghost.

Close.

"He's dead," she managed.

"Jasper?" A stupid question. Of course. Who else?

Abby swept past the girl, through the living room, dining room, into the kitchen.

There was a strange odor. Not the body; something like scorched metal.

Jasper had been stuffed into the low cabinet next to the ice maker. The one Abby, in her identical kitchen, kept her pots and pans in. The body had clearly been there a while. She backed out of the room.

"*They* came for him!" the redhead said.

"Who? What are you talking about?" Abby turned on her. "What are you even doing here?"

"Rachel sent me!"

Rachel.

"The crazy woman who lives in the camper!" Hannah clarified.

"I know," Abby said quietly.

Rachel.

Rachel DeVries.

And then Abby remembered everything.

PART THREE

THEN

—————— *1*

"So who sleeps in the cold spot?" Winter asked. She wore a translucent negligee with nothing underneath and, incongruously, bright yellow knee socks, the bottoms already black with grime. Rachel was naked. On the kitchen floor, a pentagram with flat, angular points, nestled inside a hexagon. Silver paint, accented by tall white candles at each point of each shape, eleven in all. The flickering candles threw furtive shadows in all directions; tiny, compact shadows that seemed to dart about with a life of their own before inevitably venturing too far from the light and silently perishing.

"Witty," Rachel said dismissively.

"What if she doesn't come?" Winter asked.

"She will," Rachel smiled. Double entendre.

Winter held her tongue. How do you tell someone with burn scars over a good fifth of their face and body that they're not as irresistible as they think they are? Without being a completely horrible person? You couldn't.

Besides, despite her disfigurement, Rachel *was* ridiculously sexy. If they could only bottle whatever it was that allowed her to pull it off...

They heard the front door open.

"In here!" Rachel called out.

"What if it's not her?" Winter whispered.

"Then someone's going to get the thrill of a lifetime," Rachel said, striking a pose. "If it's one of the boys, he'll probably think he's dreaming when he gets a load of us."

It wasn't one of the "boys". It was Abby.

"Where should I set up?" she managed when she picked her jaw up off the floor, mildly irritated that Rachel had managed to shock her with a little nudity and some high school satanist theatrics.

"There," Rachel said, pointing. Abby positioned the tripod she carried under her arm, checked the settings on her camera-phone, and hit REC.

"We're rolling," she said.

"Good. Are you wearing panties?"

"What?"

"Strip down to your panties." She scooped a large glass bottle off the counter and stuck it in Abby's face. "Tequila," before Abby could ask. "It'll loosen you up."

Abby took a swig, nearly gagged, forced herself to take a second. She hadn't so much as glanced at a bottle of tequila since collage.

"Are you plugged in, Winterberry?"

Winter closed her eyes. A great calm seemed to settle over her, and, by extension, the entire room. Abby felt warm and fuzzy, as if she'd been sipping the tequila all night.

"I'm in," Winter sang.

"Prove it," Rachel said.

"You're mentally unstable and disconcertingly horny, and your family once owned a dog named Biscuits that the mailman backed over in the driveway."

Rachel smiled.

"That's me."

Winter's lip twitched.

"Darker things..." the psychic said, more to herself than the others. She looked mildly distressed.

"Maybe don't dig too deep there, Winterberry."

Abby took another pull from the bottle.

"Panties," Rachel said, turning her attention back to the journalist.

Abby handed the bottle over and peeled off her shirt, then unzipped her fly. Rachel stepped forward, helped her tug off her shorts. They dropped to the floor and Abby stepped out of them.

Why did she feel so drunk, so quickly?

"It's not tequila," Rachel said, answering her unspoken question. She pressed her bare breasts against Abby's own. Abby hadn't worn a bra. "And you're not here to document this moment."

"I'm... not?" Abby whispered. Her stomach

was a knot, and her hands were shaking. Rachel's lips brushed her own, but pulled away when Abby tried to kiss them.

"No, my love. You're bait."

"I'm bait," Abby repeated, unconcerned.

"*We're* bait," Rachel clarified, and kissed her, finally.

Abby felt like she was floating, drowning. The two women sank to the floor, a tangle of arms and legs. Two of the candles were knocked over, went out. Abby struggled to remove her panties. Rachel grabbed them, roughly tore them away, then slipped two fingers inside her.

Abby tried to speak but could only groan with pleasure. She realized, vaguely, that she'd been drugged, didn't care. She only prayed this feeling would go on forever.

"Spirits of the air," Rachel said, to her, but not to her, "without a soul to care, unite with me!"

Rachel writhed beneath her, groaning.

"Spirits of the earth, vile afterbirth, unite with me!"

Winter gasped.

"You can get in on this, Winterberry," Rachel cooed. Not quite a command. "We'll ruin you for men, I promise you that much..."

"No," Winter shook her head. Terrified. "Something's coming!" Her mind touched it obliquely, a blanket of shadow descending upon the house, blotting out the moon. The enormity of its hate was incomprehensible.

"Yes! Yes!" Rachel shouted, abandoning Abby,

rolling onto her back, opening her legs, inviting it in.

"No!!!" Winter screamed, pulling out of Rachel's mind, instantaneously erecting a multitude of psychic defenses, praying they were enough, praying it hadn't perceived her. She turned, ran, passed through something cold and wet and invisible as it swept into the room.

We're all going to die, she realized, too late.

—— **2**

Shane heard someone scream, woke up, realized it was just a dream, then heard it again and realized that it wasn't. Half-falling out of the cot he'd set up in the last house on the left, and still in his boxers and a t-shirt, he bolted out the front door and stared in awe at what could only be, despite everything he'd ever believed, an honest-to-goodness ghost. Pale, ethereal, silver hair streaming behind her as she silently fled from the house at the head of the cul...

Why was she wearing yellow socks?

It wasn't a ghost. It was that goth-girl psychic, Winter, practically naked.

And the scream hadn't been hers, he realized, because he heard it again, coming from the house in question.

Someone was in trouble. He sprinted for the front door, covered most of the distance before every window in the place blew out simultaneously, the force responsible so powerful that even twenty yards away it knocked him off his feet.

3

Sandpaper. Dry ice. Razor blades. The barbed penis of a cat. Those one-way spikes in parking lots, where signs warn you not to back up. The protuberance inside Rachel was all this and more, and it was tearing her to shreds. She fought and howled and pounded against the invisible weight holding her down, to no avail. It was mutilating her, it was...

"Help me!!!!" she wailed, knowing there was no one, anywhere, who could.

There was a sudden drop in pressure, followed by a muffled explosion. Particles of glass rained down from somewhere. The kitchen window had blown out. Abby, dazed, drugged, focused on crawling away from whatever was happening. The kitchen was a maelstrom, like being in the center of a tornado, candles and clothing and debris all swirling around, balls of light appearing and expanding and flaring out like a silent fireworks display. And at the center of it, hovering two feet above the floor, thrashing and screaming in agony, Rachel DeVries.

Her Rachel.

She had to do something, she had to...

Something grabbed her wrist. No, some**one**.

Shane Whiteshroud was dragging her out of the kitchen. He scooped her up like she was weightless, carried her into the living room.

"Rachel," she managed. "We have to save Rachel from..." From what? "Herself," she decided.

Shane stared at her. His mouth opened, but nothing came out. The look in his eyes was that of a man whose mind was clearly overwhelmed, possibly broken, perhaps permanently. But he carried her outside, placed her carefully on the lawn, then turned and went back inside. The others were gathering around, some of them. They hovered, ogled, but didn't approach. Silently, she cursed them.

"Step aside." Jasper. Wearing a nightshirt and a sleeping cap, like someone in a corny old movie. He marched past her without a glance and entered the house.

—— *4*

A colicky baby. The buzzing of angry insects. Small animals in their death throes. A ringing phone, unanswerable. The house was a cacophony of unpleasant sounds, all directionless, all without source. And beneath this, Rachel's howls of agony. The walls were shaking, vibrating so hard they threatened to tear themselves apart. The air stank of rot and feces, soul-blemishing hate and that darkly glittering instant when hope finally dies.

Jasper closed his eyes. Rejected the lot of it. Denied the reality of it.

Slowly, slowly, it all went away.

Carefully, avoiding the broken glass (he was barefoot), he made his way through the dark, into the kitchen. From lifelong habit he flicked the light switch, and the light came on, illuminating the room. Quite unfortunately, he didn't think to question this. He was too distracted by the tableau before him.

Broken candles, a paganesque symbol painted on the floor, a shattered bottle of tequila, women's undergarments scattered about. He'd been to worse parties in his day. Shane, in his boxers, loomed over the naked body of Rachel, her privates and legs streaked with blood. Anyone coming upon the scene would have assumed he'd just violently assaulted her.

Jasper knew better, of course. He knelt, checked her pulse at the wrist. He'd never felt comfortable touching a person's throat. It felt too intimate; too morbid, somehow.

"She's alive," he said.

Standing, he tentatively probed the house with his mind. Nothing. But whatever had done this, it certainly hadn't fled. Likely, it was hiding.

Everything went wonky for a moment and he closed his eyes against the migraine that flared up and instantly dissipated. An attack? Ineffective, if it was. He felt suddenly fatigued, as if he'd been on his feet for hours.

"We probably shouldn't move her," he went on, aloud. "But the only other option is for someone to drive towards the highway until they get a signal, then call 911 and hope they can direct the responders in without getting them lost. Better we take her ourselves. Can you lift her, Mr. Whiteshroud?" He looked to the Indian. Shane's eyes were glassy, far away. "Mr. Whiteshroud!"

"Huh?" Shane looked at Jasper like he was

seeing him for the first time. Apparently, shattering his worldview so utterly and dramatically had somewhat distressed him. Well, there was no time for that now.

"Pick up Ms. DeVries and bring her outside. I'll have someone pull a car up to the door!"

Shane nodded absently as Jasper scampered outside.

"Who's got the most...?" he began as he burst out the front door. He froze.

Everyone else was... gone.

<h1>—— 5</h1>

Music and laughter radiated in waves from the house next door. Had they lost their minds? Jasper raced over and ran face-first into the door when he tried to burst through it. It was locked.

"Open up!" he shouted, pounding. There was a click and the door swung open.

Buffy. Emily, rather. One of Mahmoud's tart assistants. She had a bottle of beer in her hand.

"We'll turn it down," she said, vaguely irritated.

"What?"

"The music. We'll turn it down."

"What? No, I need a car!" Jasper sputtered. Emily stared at him like he'd just sprouted a second head, and it told her to move to Dallas.

"So buy one," she said.

"Have you lost your...?!?" he began.

She closed the door. The lock clicked into place. A moment later, the music was turned down. Slightly.

He looked up and down the street, really taking it in.

There were lights on in most of the houses. Real lights, as if they had power. The vehicles had all been moved, neatly slotted into drives or, in the case of the RV, carefully parked curbside.

What in God's name was happening?

Motion, to his right. Shane Whiteshroud was purposefully lumbering up the middle of the street, carrying the unconscious Rachel DeVries in his arms. Like the Mummy in an old Universal picture. Jasper lost sight of them behind the mass of foliage sprouting out of the nearest traffic island, foliage greener and thicker than he remembered it being.

He ran after.

"Wait!" he shouted. "Wait!"

Shane carried her through the front door of one of the houses across the street. Dark, this one, but a moment later a light came on.

Dark thoughts, carefully crafted to manipulate him, sprouted unbidden in his brain.

He's going to assault her.

He took her someplace private to assault her.

An unconscious, injured girl.

I have to stop him.

I'll find something.

Something heavy.

Bash.

Bash his brains in.

No.

It, whatever **it** was, was toying with his mind, manipulating his perceptions. From hiding. And he knew where it was hiding. Inside the girl. The foolish, mad girl who had invited it in.

Well, there was only one thing to do.

He'd have to kill her.

$$—— 6$$

Shane stared dully as Jasper burst through the doorway. He'd placed Rachel carefully on a dining room table that shouldn't have been there, neatly set for one. The plates and silverware matched the sets Jasper had at home, although he didn't notice this. Scooping up a cloth napkin, Jasper held it tightly over Rachel's nose and mouth, pinching the latter.

He wasn't really going to kill her, of course. But he needed the entity inside of her – be it demon or ghost or wayward spirit traveler – to believe that he would, to panic and flee before its host died, which would cause him/her/them/it great discomfort, at the very least.

Rachel tried to gasp, struggled.

"Come out, come out," Jasper urged, "or it's really going to hurt. Or maybe you'll be stuck in there, possessing an inanimate corpse forever."

Rachel's eyes suddenly opened, wide, filled

with panic. She struggled, scratched his face, then gripped his wrist tightly with both hands and almost managed to pull his suffocating pressure away.

"I'm not playing," Jasper said calmly. "I know you're in there."

"Almost right," Shane said dully, and plunged the steak knife he'd palmed into Jasper's back, up to the hilt.

Shit, Jasper thought as he let go of the girl, hopelessly clawing for the knife protruding from between his shoulder blades. Simultaneously, Rachel kicked him, hard, in the stomach, doubling him over. He dropped to his knees as she rolled off the table onto the floor. Without waiting to see what happened next she crawled into the kitchen, out the back door. Pulling herself to her feet she found she could walk, although it hurt terribly, and stumbled around to the front of the house.

The RV was parked at the curb, in front of the next house over.

The keys. That idiot Arab always left the keys in the ignition. Please let them be there now.

They were.

She climbed inside, vaguely noted the dog darting out between her legs.

If this were a bad movie, the engine wouldn't turn over.

But it wasn't, and it did.

She threw the RV into gear. It jerked forward, but she quickly got it under control and gunned it, heart pounding as the huge, cumbersome vehicle took forever, creeping down the street, around the corner, and onto the service road, where it finally picked up speed.

——— *7*

Shane stabbed Jasper again and again and again and again. Dozens of times. Hundreds. Too many to count. At one point, for reasons he didn't quite understand, he started singing "I'm a Believer", by the Monkees. Finally, he grew bored. He became aware of a piercing, irritating sound. A small dog, running in circles, barking and nipping at him. He considered stabbing the dog, too, but he was tired of stabbing. From the corner of the room Jasper watched, jaw agape, as Shane stuffed the soggy, broken mess of a corpse into the cabinet next to the ice maker. It wouldn't *quite* fit, so Shane roughly stomped it into the space with his right foot.

"Go away," the thing inside Shane told the lingering spirit. Jasper wasn't moving on. He was in total denial, the notion of his own death an unthinkable impossibility, and so he himself had become one of the confused spirits that he'd so often coaxed into the light.

"I'm going to bed," Jasper said instead. "Everything will be fine in the morning." Dismissing the grisly sight before him, he shuffled out of the room as if in a daze, unhurriedly mounted the stairs. The little dog whined once, growled at Shane, then reluctantly followed.

"They'll come for you, soon enough," Shane said. He forced the cabinet door until the latch caught.

$$\underline{\hspace{3cm}} \; 8$$

Abby, still naked, stood on her second floor balcony, gin and tonic in one hand, cigarette in the other, and watched impassively as Shane – a complete stranger to her – burst out Jasper's front door, paused, reeled around the front yard for several seconds, and then dropped to his knees in the middle of the street. After a time, he looked up and caught sight of her. Vaguely aware of her nudity, she subtly struck a pose. *Who am I?* she wondered even as she did this. *Should I be mortified?*

She was certain she'd know by morning.

For the moment, she was only mildly concerned when the man in the street pointed right at her, as if calling her out, and then let out an ululating wail that sounded more like the cry of a wounded animal than the scream of a man. It just didn't seem that important.

She wasn't even fazed when the RV that had

pulled out several seconds earlier careened back around the corner, blasted Shane, and continued into the cul, finally jumping the curb at the head of the street (blowing out a tire in the process), continuing on through the yard, and an isolated length of fence, then disappearing into the pre-dawn fog that had temporarily claimed the undeveloped land beyond. She looked down at Shane's mangled, broken body impassively. Someone would have to clean that up, she noted, before snubbing out her cigarette and retreating inside.

The street lights, fully functional now, flickered off at the kiss of the rising sun. The fog reluctantly burned away. The earliest risers rolled out of bed, yawned, stretched, showered and brushed teeth and dutifully prepared for work, or school, or simply enjoyed their morning coffee before venturing out to seize the day.

Everyone who wasn't dead, was home.

PART FOUR

NOW

—— *1*

Why did Rachel turn around?

Why didn't she drive straight to a hospital, or come back with the National Guard?

In remembering, Abby felt like she'd unearthed more questions than answers.

The redhead with the boy-cut – Hannah – was staring at her, eyes silently pleading with her to make some sort of decision.

"Okay," Abby said. "Take me to her."

"Hello, Rachel."

The RV was a shambles, and it stank. Most of the tires were flat, Abby had noted as they approached. Rachel wasn't looking much better. Disheveled, perfunctorily dressed, she moved as if she were in pain. Something internal.

"I told you to bring the flamer psychic," she told Hannah. She didn't even look at Abby.

"He's dead," Abby said.

"I heard he wasn't."

"Fake news." Abby turned to Hannah. "Could you give us a minute?"

Hannah stepped outside, closed the door, then pressed an ear against it to listen.

"You used me," Abby said.

"I use everybody. And I paid for it. That thing tore me up inside. I'm no good for anything now. That was all I had left and it *took* it from me. So I paid the fucking piper. Go ahead and gloat, like you never did anything wrong, never fucked anybody over. Stupid hypocrite bitch."

Abby reached out, touched Rachel's cheek.

"Don't touch me," Rachel said, pulling away. "I told you I'm no good. I can't feel anything."

"Not even here?" Abby indicated her heart. Rachel snorted.

"Did you just stroll down the side of Walton's Mountain? Give me a break."

"Why'd you come back, then?"

"Revenge, obviously. Winter, it didn't get Winter. We've been cooking something up."

"Why didn't you just go to the cops?"

"And tell them what?"

"Fair point." Abby sighed. "Well, we're four now, if you'll have us."

The RV door opened before Rachel could respond.

"I'm not helping you with *anything* unless we solve *my* problem first!" Hannah exclaimed.

"What is your problem?" Abby asked.

"Men," Rachel answered for her.

——— *3*

"First, we'll need Winter," Rachel had said. Abby agreed to collect her, alone. They didn't want to arouse the... *neighborhood's*... suspicions by roaming around in an increasingly sizable group.

The houses seemed duller, washed out, now that her thoughts were her own again. And somehow unreal, like she'd stepped out of one dream and into another, less intense but with subtle dangers all its own. The sounds of construction, omnipresent over the last few weeks, had vanished. She couldn't see from where she currently stood, at the head of the cul, but she suspected that, for her at least, the men and equipment and partially constructed units surrounding them had vanished. Did they have any objective reality at all, she wondered? If enough people believed in them, would they, then, become real?

The thought brought an involuntary shudder.

She knocked on Winter's front door. Winter... and Itsuki, she remembered. In the nightmare-dream the neighborhood had weaved, they were husband and wife.

Itsuki answered the door. He appeared vaguely irritated, as if she'd interrupted him at something unimportant, but still more important that whatever she might want.

"Yes?" he said.

"Is Winter home?" she asked. Were they friends in the fantasy world the neighborhood had created? Did they even know each other? Already, she couldn't remember.

"Come in," Itsuki said, in a dead, neutral tone that strongly suggested to her that she shouldn't.

"I'll swing by later," she said instead, taking a step back. He kept one of his hands behind his back, overtly out of sight. What was he hiding?

"No. Come in."

She backpedaled until she was halfway to the street.

"No, it's okay. I'll come back later."

Itsuki's lip twitched. Without a word, he slowly closed the door. As he did so, Abby caught a glimpse of the long, gleaming French cook knife, clenched behind his back in a death grip.

—— *4*

Using gasoline siphoned from the RV, Rachel set Ahmad's body on fire, right there in the middle of the field. This served a dual purpose: technically appeasing Hannah, while also shocking and intimidating her. Rachel always believed in offing multiples with one stone.

"Should we... should we say a prayer or something?" Hannah managed after the smoldering mass had reached a point where it was no longer recognizable as a person.

"I don't know any Muslim prayers," Rachel said.

Someone was coming, making a beeline for them across the field. Abby. Rachel frowned. She was alone.

"Winter?" Rachel asked.

Abby shrugged.

They stood in silence for several seconds, trying not to look at the smoldering body, trying not to look at each other.

"I wonder what would happen," Abby finally said, "if someone just strolled into one of those houses, turned on the gas, and lit a match?"

"Winter tried that," Rachel said. "Used the stove and then left the gas on 'by accident'. After a few minutes it just shut itself off. Then a window opened, all by itself, to let the accumulated gas out. And to show off, maybe. Prove its point."

"You make it sound like they're alive," Hannah said. "The houses." She almost said *our* houses, but caught herself. "That's crazy."

"They are alive, missy. In a sense. They're *inhabited*. Every board, every tile, every nail and appliance and lamp and piece of furniture. It, they, can manipulate its materials and furnishings the same way we manipulate an arm or a leg. You see? It's a part of them, body to their soul."

"You learned all this by fucking one?" Abby asked coolly.

"Winter explained it to me," Rachel said. She strove to keep her tone neural. She didn't appreciate Abby's flip attitude, but wasn't about to give her the satisfaction.

"But what if we introduced something from outside?" Abby pondered. "Could it control that?"

"It controlled us," Hannah reminded her.

"But not right away. Maybe things have to... I don't know, acclimate to it?"

"It's a thought," Rachel conceded.

"What were you thinking of introducing from outside?" Hannah asked. "A nuclear bomb?"

Abby smiled.

"Kind of."

———— **5**

Big Guy frowned. The RV that had pulled in was riding on at least two rims, and the woman pumping the gas was his crazy semi-regular. The woman paying for the gas was something else altogether. In addition to the gasoline, she'd cleaned him out of propane, kerosene, lighter fluid, *and* fireworks, and given the scarring on her arm and face she didn't look like someone who should be playing with any of those things. Now his semi-regular was filling up unapproved containers with gasoline – including a plastic dish tub and a little wastepaper basket – and a third girl was stashing these inside the RV. He wondered, briefly, if he should call the cops – or at least the fire department – but ultimately decided against it. Better not to get involved.

———— 6

"I grew up around propane," Abby explained, hefting one of the grill tanks for emphasis, "and you can't blow one of these up by dropping it or shooting it with a gun. That's a misconception." The other two were rapt with attention. A little *too* rapt in Rachel's case, Abby thought. They were back in the fields behind the cul, the RV parked a hundred yards away, its door and windows propped open to ease the overpowering stench of gasoline. "You can, however, blow them up by heating them externally. Say, in a house fire. The tank heats up and the gas inside becomes too pressurized, which triggers the safety valve. Gas is released, ignites, heats the tank even more... a vicious cycle. Eventually, this results in a BLEVE – a Boiling Liquid, Expanding Vapor Explosion. Basically an expanding ball of fire, seasoned with shrapnel from the compromised tank."

Rachel applauded enthusiastically.

"We'll be placing these, surreptitiously, in strategic locations inside each house. Ditto our containers of gas. Then we slather the place with lighter fluid and light it from a distance with one of these." Abby set down the grill tank and held up a roman candle. Though the cardboard tube was meant to be placed on the ground, it could easily be held in the hand when lit and then discharged in any direction. Not exactly safe, but effective.

"My brother and his friends used to have fireworks wars with those," Hannah pointed out. "They'd literally run around the neighborhood, shooting exploding balls of fire at each other. It's a wonder no one got hurt."

"So it'll work," Abby said.

"What if someone asks us what we're doing?" Rachel asked. "Like, 'Excuse me? Why are you splashing gasoline all over my house?'"

"We'll prep the empty houses first. Mine, Jasper's, Hannah's. Maybe we'll get lucky and someone else will be out and we can get a fourth one staged too. We'll run gas trails to the others if we can. Should be plenty of chaos when several houses go up all at once. We'll hit the remainder then, hard and fast. With any luck, the whole fucking neighborhood will burn."

"I think I love you," Rachel said.

————— 7

It was slow work, in no small part because of the subterfuge involved. Wandering back and forth from the RV to one house, that house to the next, stashing a propane tank here, a jug of gasoline there. The larger, open containers full of gasoline proved wholly impractical to move, and Rachel ended up emptying them into the little RV bathtub, nearly filling it. They were loath to discard it, in case they needed it later. And through it all, a strange tenseness in the air. Nerves? Or something else?

Once the three inarguably empty houses were primed, Abby and Hannah began calling on their neighbors. Bobbi was home. Emily and Madison were not. Lionel appeared to be in, but didn't answer his door.

That left Itsuki.

"I don't know if I can maintain, knowing Winter's probably dead in there," Hannah said.

"We'll hit him last," Abby decided.

The pair broke in through Emily and Madison's back door, placed a propane tank on the dining room table, then piled everything flammable they could find on top of it and soaked the pile in accelerant. Hannah opened the dining room window that looked out onto the back yard.

Abby took a deep breath.

"Okay. This one first, then I'll do a lap and light up the other three. You fetch Rachel. I want you two to drive that RV right through the narrow side of Lionel's yard and into the middle of the street. That'll put you equidistant from two of the three houses we haven't prepped. Got it?"

Hannah nodded.

"Okay. Go."

She went.

Abby extracted a roman candle and a disposable lighter from her front sweatshirt pocket.

There was a muffled cry, a brief scuffle outside.

"Abby!" Hannah. Suddenly cut off.

Oh shit.

Abby burst through the kitchen door, into the back yard.

Hannah was on her knees, one arm twisted behind her back, Lionel's hand over her mouth. Next to him, Madison, the brunette, curiously examining the roman candle she'd taken out of Hannah's pocket.

"I smell kerosene," Lionel said. He spoke like

177

he was reading a cue card in a foreign language. Sounding it out phonetically.

"You were gonna use this?" Madison asked Abby, holding up the firework. "Make a boom-boom?"

"Let her go," Abby said.

"You sound like a pulp novel," Lionel said without inflection.

"Yeah, one of those." Madison had Hannah's lighter, too. She flicked it, lit the roman candle's fuse. Jesus Christ, was she going to light up the house herself?

No.

She forced the business end of the roman candle into Hannah's mouth. Lionel had both of the redhead's arms now and he held her tight, kept her from moving. She winced, her eyes filling with tears.

"Jesus Christ, don't!" Abby pleaded.

"There are worse holes I could've stuck it in," Madison smiled. Her tone, unlike Lionel's, could have passed for natural. In fact, she seemed to be enjoying herself.

A third of the fuse had sparkle-danced away.

"I surrender," Abby said, dropping her own firework, and lighter.

Half the fuse.

"Did I ask you to surrender?"

Three quarters.

"For God's sake!" Abby screamed.

"He has nothing to do with this," Madison said. At the last possible moment she pulled the roman candle out of Hannah's mouth and pointed it at Abby's face.

—— *8*

Abby got her arms up just in time. The shell exploded against them, peppering her partially-shielded face with pinpoints of purple fire, but it was nowhere near as bad as she would've expected. The belated flash-and-bang was the worst part – visible even behind closed eyes, and now she couldn't see, or hear. She lunged forward anyway, hoping to get hold of Madison, but ended up on the ground, flat on her face. A closed fist struck the back of her head, hard. So hard that, despite not being able to see anything else, she saw stars. *Funny,* she thought, *I always assumed that was just a lazy metaphor.*

Oblivion welcomed her with open arms, and she was glad for it.

9

She was being dragged by her hair. Over concrete. She opened her eyes. Something wrong... too dark. Oblivion was much more pleasant, so she nestled back into it. Just five more minutes...

10

She came to, fully, arms numb from lack of circulation, the world around her dull and grey. She was standing, lashed to something with belts and strips of cloth. A tree! One of the trees jutting angrily out of the patch of earth afforded them on one of the center islands. And it was dark, nighttime dark. But it wasn't nighttime. Banks of clouds, deep grey as to be nearly black, had rolled in, blotting out the sun. Blotting out the entire world.

Hannah was tied to a tree on the other center island. The others were all there – Madison, Emily, Lionel, Itsuki, Robert and Roberta. Was that it? Was everyone else dead?

"Good morning," Madison said. Their mouthpiece. And yet, Abby sensed that it could have been any one of them. Like they shared a mind. "Welcome to the first day of the new world."

"Get out of them, you evil shit!" Abby spat.

Madison cocked her head, confused. Like a dog that had been given contradictory commands.

"You ignorant, fleshy worm. Your 'evil' is a meaningless concept. 'Demons' you theorize, or 'ghosts'. You don't understand the first of it. You couldn't *hope* to understand."

"Screw you!" Hannah contributed.

"Glory in your fortune," Madison said dryly, "as you burn for..." She coughed up several incomprehensible syllables that sounded more like clicks and hisses than words.

The twins approached Hannah, doused her in lighter fluid. She spat and swore as it got in her mouth and eyes.

There was a sound, Abby realized, underlying everything. Something approaching.

The others looked around. It *wasn't* her imagination. Something was coming in hard, behind them, behind the house at the head of the cul. Something that growled and whined.

It careened out from between the houses, massive and low and trailing flame.

The RV.

And it was on fire.

The undercarriage screamed in protest as it bounced over the curb, bottomed out on the concrete, and made a beeline for the crowd, trailing sparks, striking Itsuki and hurling him high into the air even as the others scattered. Already, the flames were sputtering out.

Accelerant, coating the outer body and set alight. The great beast bore on, continuing to accelerate until it plunged into the front of Hannah's house, across the street, to a cacophony of crunching fiberglass and cracking wood and exploding glass. A lone hubcap, lost in the leap over the curb, rolled after it like an eager sycophant, until it hit the opposite curb, bounced off, and toppled over.

The driver side door burst open and a figure fell out.

Rachel.

Climbing to her feet, she produced a roman candle from somewhere on her person, lit it.

Abby was cheering and she didn't even realize it.

The shutters on the front of Hannah's house – those that hadn't been compromised in the crash – began flapping wildly, opening and closing so hard that they slammed against the outer wall, splintering the facade. Upstairs, the quarter moon attic windows flashed as if a light were being turned rapidly on and off in the room beyond. Everything that was a part of the house that could move did move, fluttering and flailing as if in a panic.

As if it were... afraid.

"Die," Rachel said, and lit it up.

There was no explosion, and it wasn't even especially dramatic, but it caught, and the fire spread quickly, feeding on the flammables and remnants of accelerant they'd staged earlier.

Turning, Rachel marched – with a noticeable limp – towards Abby and Hannah. She had a whole string of roman candles, strung over her shoulder like a bandoleer.

The others were already recovering. One of them hissed, like an angry serpent. The sound was so inhuman that Abby cringed inwardly. Rachel had reached Hannah, passed her, came to Abby first. She planted a long, lingering kiss on Abby as she tore her free.

Hannah's house was burning freely now.

And it was *screaming*.

Abby accepted the lighter and two of the fireworks from Rachel, lit both fuses, and fired them alternately at the Remingtons, Lionel, and the other two girls. They swam through the barrage, but it gave Rachel time to free Hannah. Itsuki hadn't moved since he'd crashed back to earth, and given the amount of blood pooling around his head, likely he never would.

The entire world was the stench of gunpowder, ringing ears, and after-images of yellow and purple fire blooming in the air.

"Go, damn it!" someone shouted.

They ran.

—— *11*

Abby's sight had fully returned, but now her chest hurt from sprinting the length of the neighborhood. She found herself in front of Jasper's house, stopped, fumbled for the fresh firework Rachel tossed her, dropped it, picked it up. Hannah, behind them, went down, tackled to the ground by Buffy. Emily, rather. Abby was pummeled by an overpowering urge, very nearly a distinct voice in her head:

Just keep running, Get out. Escape. Flee this place and never look back.

No.

It had gone too far for that.

She turned, ran through Jasper's front door, froze.

The place still stank of accelerant, a conflagration waiting to happen.

But somewhere, in her flight down the street, she lost her lighter.

The kitchen!

She ran to the back of the house, tried not to look at the remnants of Jasper, now lolling out of the cabinet by the ice maker. She triggered one of the burners on the gas store and a ring of blue flame leapt to life.

And promptly sputtered out.

The house knew what she was trying to do, and was moving to prevent it.

From behind her, a howl/shriek, like a wounded, hateful animal.

She spun around.

Robert, facing her, his mouth open so wide that the sides were bloody, torn. The sound that came out was like nothing she'd ever heard, ever imagined. He lunged for her and she dodged, wincing as his clumsy assault took him head-first into the counter with an organic *crack*. He grabbed the counter to keep from falling down but she kicked him in the back of the leg, hard, so that he went down anyway, then pressed her attack, kicking and stomping as he struggled to rise. She was winning!

Right up to the moment when Roberta grabbed her from behind.

The two women dance-struggled backwards, into the dining room, knocking several depleted bottles of lighter fluid and an accelerant-soaked throw pillow off the table, toppling a chair, finally falling to the floor in a flailing heap. Abby grabbed a handful of Roberta's hair, pulling until a fistful came out, then got the twin in a headlock and rolled over on top of her.

At the far end of the street there was a muffled explosion.

Jasper's entire house briefly shuddered. In sympathy? Or was it afraid?

Robert grabbed Abby from behind, pulled her off his sibling.

One of Abby's flailing hands closed on a bottle of lighter fluid. She swung it around, squeezed. The minimal remnants inside speckled Robert's face, got in his eyes. He cried out, released her.

Roberta was already climbing to her feet. Weaponizing a handy table lamp, she tore it out of the wall with so much force that there was a brief shower of sparks.

Brief, but it was enough.

Half the room was aflame before any of them realized what had happened.

"No, my love!" Robert shouted, pushing Abby aside in his haste to reach his sister, already engulfed. A moment later, *"My face!!!!"* Abby crawled into the kitchen, climbed unsteadily to her feet, nearly fell out the kitchen door into the back yard. Something hot licked her back and she realized she was on fire so she stopped, dropped, and rolled until she'd snuffed it out.

Behind her, inside, the crackling of flames, and screams, and the stink of cooking meat.

———— *12*

Three houses were on fire now – Jasper's, Hannah's, and her own. Clearly Rachel had lit up the third. But where was Rachel? And where was everyone else? Hannah was a crumpled mass in the middle of the street. Rachel went to her. She'd been badly beaten – Emily hadn't done this. Lionel? Was he even still alive? She wracked her brain, reeling at the bald, nightmarish fact that she was trying to remember who, in their sizable group, was still alive.

Her, Hannah, and Rachel (hopefully).

Opposing: Lionel, Madison, and Emily.

Even odds. They might walk away from this yet.

Carefully lifting Hannah in her arms (she was heavier than she looked), Abby carried her to her car, currently parked a safe distance from "her" house, and gently placed her in the back seat. By now said house was an inferno, and she reflected how unfortunate it would be if she'd left her keys inside. Fortunately, she hadn't. Across the street, thick smoke was pouring out of the broken windows and open front door of the twins' place. The sizable paperweight and tiny end table that had been hurled through the windows rested incongruously on the front lawn. Well, now she knew where Rachel was.

There was a low keening coming from somewhere, she realized, like an angry teakettle. Several instances of this, actually. The houses' death knell? She hoped so.

"Hey!" Rachel, strolling out of the twins' house. Hesitant flames were joining the smoke now, dancing behind the broken panes of glass. "Three to go."

"Get in," Abby said, slipping behind the wheel. Rachel did, and kissed her, and it seemed congratulatory and perfunctory at first but suddenly they were lost in it, lips tingling, the world receding. Abby broke it off, before someone – or something – snuck up on them while they were swimming in bliss.

"Oh my God," Hannah said. She'd come to her senses, was staring past them through the windshield. "What is *that?*" The other two women followed her gaze.

At the far end of the street, proceeding in a line out the front door of Lionel's house... madness.

Furniture. Tables and chairs and a desk. An ottoman. A floor lamp. Walking. No, marching, as if to war, their legs facilitating this by pivoting and bending in ways that their construction couldn't possibly account for. An army – or a squad, anyway – of inanimate objects, on the go, coming for them.

It reminded Abby of a short story she'd read as a child, its particulars lost to time.

"We could just back up," Rachel suggested. "Get the hell out of here."

"No," Abby said. "We're finishing this."

Hannah nodded in assent.

Abby stomped on the gas.

—————— *13*

Most of the cheap furniture exploded into splinters as they plowed through it, and Abby cut left, avoiding the large, cumbersome writing desk entirely. Rachel tumbled out even before the car had come to a complete stop, pulled Hannah out behind her, shoved a grill lighter into her hands, and pushed her in the direction of Emily and Madison's, which she and Abby had prepped earlier but never got the chance to set ablaze. Already, the surviving furniture had turned around and was jauntily marching after them.

"You do Winter's, I'll do Lionel's!" Rachel said.

"We don't have any more accelerant!" Abby pointed out.

A muffled explosion, down the street, punctuated this. One of the propane tanks finally going up.

"Just light up anything flammable! That's what I did at incest central and it's burning just fine!"

The Brownies wouldn't award me my campfire badge because I couldn't get my damn fire going, and look at me now, Abby thought as she burst through the front door. Using her lighter, and the roman candles Rachel had given her, she set fire to everything in sight. Tablecloth. Blanket. A loose book lying open on the desk. Boxes in the pantry. Sheaves of paperwork. Even the toilet paper in the bathroom, which had been hung the wrong way, she noted. In a modern home this never would have worked – too many flame-resistant products. But here... this place seemed to exist perpetually in the 1970s. It was easy.

"Bitch!!!" someone shrieked.

Oh oh.

She spun around, ducked instinctively just as something whizzed through the space where her head had been. It was Emily, wielding the only weapon she could find, a hand saw. She swung wildly, aiming for Abby's noggin, and missed again as Abby danced backwards, out of her reach.

*"You're ruining everything you're killing **everything**!!!!!!!!"* the girl screamed, her eyes wild with madness.

"Emily! Emily, listen to me!" Abby tried. Walking backwards, eyes glued on her assailant, the inevitable happened.

She tripped.

Emily was a tiny little thing, really, and yet

now she loomed over Abby like the end of the world.

"I'm going to plant this in your face and then saw and saw until half of your head comes off," she growled.

The house around them was starting to burn, reluctantly, but nevertheless there was suddenly a unique smell in the air. Something burning, but different. Pungent, harsh, something that...

"My hair!" Emily screamed, dropping the saw and batting at the back of her head. Hands roughly pushed her aside.

It was Hannah. Hannah had crept up behind and set her hair on fire. Abby scrambled to her feet and made for the door, pulling Hannah behind when she hesitated, belatedly realized what she had done, and to who. They fell out the front door and onto the lawn. Emily was right behind them, howling, a halo of fire around her head. Abby managed to get to her feet, run her down, tackle her in the neighboring yard and rub her head in the dirt until the fire was out. "What's happening? What's happening?!" she was screaming. But it was all confusion and terror. She'd have to cut most of her hair off, but she hadn't been seriously injured.

"Look out!" Hannah screamed as Abby was processing this, just before something kicked her in the head. Rolling over and sitting up, she found herself face to... face?... with a folding bamboo chair, dancing and gallivanting in front of her like a boxer trying to draw in a strike.

Impossibly, one of its legs kicked at her again, a feint. Hannah strode up to it, grabbed it from behind, and hurled it high into the air. It landed with a harsh *crack* and remained motionless. The other animate household items had disappeared. Abby imagined them running off, escaping, to live quiet, resentful lives elsewhere in neglected thrift stores or unused spare bedrooms.

"Is it over?" Hannah asked while Abby comforted the sobbing blonde.

No, it wasn't, Abby realized. Where was Rachel?

As if in response, a skull-grinding creaking and fracturing, of distressed wood and compromised concrete, threatened to drown out everything.

The three women turned in its direction, as one.

"Oh my God," two of them said simultaneously.

What the third one said is unprintable.

14

Lionel's house, the only one not engulfed in flames, was *moving*. Not walking, exactly, for of course it had no legs, but rather scuffling, and sliding, lifting first one corner – ripped from its own foundation – then the other, and slowly pulling itself towards them. The third floor windows flickered with anger – red, as if announcing itself a house of ill repute.

Jesus Christ, Abby thought. Rachel is *inside* that thing.

A metallic pop as a compromised pipe was torn free, a negligible stream of water briefly spurting into the air where the downstairs bathroom once sat. The front door flew off its hinges, flipping end over end through the air, landing just a few yards away. A great guttural growl issued forth from the darkness behind that expelled door, a growl one might hear from a cornered animal.

"Rachel!!!" Abby screamed.

"We have to get out of here!" Hannah shouted.

"No!" Abby said. "Rachel..."

"And Madison," Emily suddenly interjected. "Where's Madison?"

"Right here."

Madison was draped over the hood of Abby's car, striking a pose, grinning. There was something that might have been an ice pick in her hand. Three of Abby's tires were flat.

"Oopsie," Madison said, sliding off the hood. She put one of her fingers in her mouth and adopted a contrived, guilty little girl look. "Did I do a boo-boo?"

"God damn you," Abby hissed.

Behind them, glacially, the house moved closer.

"Oops, I missed one," Madison cooed, plunging her tool into the final tire.

Except this one exploded, propelling the metal pick backwards, into the air.

And right into her throat.

"Gak," Madison said, her eyes wide, arterial blood spraying out of her neck. She dropped to her knees, seemed to experience a moment of confused clarity, and then fell face-first to the street.

15

We could be forgiven, Abby thought, *for believing that we were literally in Hell.* Clouds blacker than a starless night roiling overhead, corpses all around them, massive pyres whipping licks of flame hundreds of feet into the air. Near-distant, muffled explosions. Emily screaming. And now Rachel, too, was gone, likely consumed by the impossible *thing* that was slowly, inexorably bearing down on them. The thing that couldn't be alive, yet was alive. An inescapable melancholia settled over her, enveloped her. They were grains of sand – no, less than that – battered about by an incomprehensible, uncaring universe. How was it worse to lay down and die rather than fight, when fighting brought only more loss, more pain? Was this sudden defeatism her own, or was it impressed upon her by something else, something outside of her? If the latter, was it really any less valid?

"Look!" Hannah said, breaking the spell.

The RV. It was moving, jerkily backing out of the flaming facade it was embedded in. Finally tearing free, it backed up, front rims bare, the tires having melted away. The windshield was gone, the entire front quarter blackened from smoke and soot, but it was in motion, jerkily swinging around so that the nose pointed towards the entrance to the cul. Towards freedom.

Behind the wheel, Rachel.

The untethered house lurched forward, shutters flapping wildly, upstairs windows flashing. Abby could feel the pull as it sucked air into the hole where the front door used to be.

Like it was inhaling.

"Come on!" she shouted, pulling Emily to her feet, making for the RV. Hannah quickly followed.

Then froze, as did the others, as Rachel hit the gas and left them behind.

"She's leaving us!!!" Hannah screamed after the retreating vehicle. "No!!!"

No, Abby realized. No, indeed.

"Get out of the way!" she cried, grabbing both girls and roughly shoving them onto the nearest traffic island, into the copse of trees. At the end of the block Rachel slammed on the brakes, so hard that she fishtailed, then made a sloppy K turn, revved the engine once, then barreled back down the street, weaving, barely under control, bare rims throwing off sparks, faster and faster until she plowed right into the impossible, free-roaming house... into and very nearly through. Abby closed her eyes, ducked, covered her head, fully anticipating an explosion. But none came. Instead, the house, already compromised from having torn itself off of its own foundation, canted ominously, wailed like an animal in its death throes, and then collapsed, the entire first floor disappearing as the second dropped several feet to replace it, beams bending and snapping and shards of masonry hurtling in every direction.

The other six houses continued to burn. The jet black clouds continued to amass (in less than an hour it would rain, a deluge, dousing the fires). There was still the occasional, isolated explosion as the last of the propane tanks went off. And yet it was as if a weight had been lifted, a presence dispelled, normalcy restored.

Abby took a deep breath, and didn't even care that she got a lungful of smoke.

Now it was over.

———— *16*

Hannah thought that they'd talk to each other through a pane of soundproof glass, via little phones mounted on the wall. Like on TV. Instead, she was led to a large, utilitarian room where Abby was seated at a small table, waiting for her. They sat across from each other. The only other prisoner in the room was a teenaged Asian girl, who glowered belligerently at the weeping mother who'd come to see her.

"How you holdin' up?" Hannah asked.

"I'm okay," Abby said. "Really," she quickly added. "I've got a lot of time to think."

"And that's good?"

Abby shrugged. "Did they charge you with anything?" she asked. Hannah nodded.

"Just property stuff, so far," she said. "Same as you. I'm out on bail. My parents." She flushed, embarrassed by the comparative perks of her economic status.

"I'm glad."

"They want to help," Hannah quickly added. "I told them you saved my life. I told them..." She paused, looked around. "Can they hear us in here?" she asked.

"I don't think so. And anyway I don't think anything they did hear would be admissible as evidence."

"Oh." Hannah lowered her voice anyway. "So, my lawyer says that blaming – 'assigning', he calls it – the murders on one of the people who died is our best bet. We just need to make sure we keep our stories straight. So he wants to take over your case, too. My parents said they'd pay for it."

"Okay," Abby said.

She reached out and Hannah took her hand. Hannah half expected the semi-attentive guard on duty to admonish them. "No touching!" But that didn't happen.

"Any news of Lionel?" Abby asked. She hesitated. "Or... Rachel?"

Hannah shook her head. They'd searched the wreckage of the final house, right up until the fire trucks began to arrive. Rachel had simply vanished. Lionel, too. Abby couldn't help but picture him holing up in one of her conjectural thrift stores, playing endless games of rummy with the animated chairs.

"So you're on board?" Hannah asked.

"Absolutely."

"Boss." Hannah stood. Their time was almost

up. "The attorney's name is Derek Michaels. He'll be in touch."

"I'll be out of here in no time," Abby smiled.

"Count on it," Hannah said.

Outside, a car was waiting for her, the engine running. She slid into the passenger seat.

"How is she?" Rachel asked, pulling out and merging carefully into traffic.

"She's okay. She asked about you."

"Did she?" Rachel didn't smile, but Hannah could hear the smile in her voice.

"You should write to her, or something."

"I will. When I've earned it. I've got a lot to atone for first."

"You're not a bad person. You deserve to be happy." Hannah said this, and she believed it.

In time, Rachel believed it too.

EPILOGUE

Winter and Itsuki's house, the last to burn, was also the first to be put out by the combined efforts of the local FD and mother nature. As such, it was the one least gutted by fire, nearest to whole, and it was here that the awareness coalesced, slowly, gathering strength over many days until its cognizance, at least, was as concrete as ever. It was crippled horribly, of course, physically unsound, uninhabitable.

Down but not out, one might say.

Because it had a plan. It *always* had a plan.

The entity occupying the house concentrated all of its attention on the ice maker in the kitchen. Scuffed and dented, scored with fire, door torn from its hinges, it nevertheless remained functional. The entity giggled to itself as the machine produced its first cube of ice, which bounced off the bottom of the bin and landed on the hardwood floor with a satisfying *clunk*. This was followed by a second, a third, a fourth. The entity giggled again, then laughed out loud, a horrific sound, like incisors dragged across a chalkboard. It would fill the *world* with ice, crowd mankind out, freeze him to *death!* A new ice age, one cube at a time!

Clunk. Clunk. Clunk.

Already, the first cubes were rapidly melting in the sweltering Florida heat.

ABOUT THE AUTHOR

Brad D. Sibbersen does not believe in ghosts, even though there's one behind you right now.